The Verona Exchange

The Verona Exchange, a Rainee Allen mystery

Printed in the United States of America

*****

Disclaimer: This is a work of fiction, a product of the author's imagination. Any resemblance or similarity to any actual events or persons, living or dead, is purely coincidental. Although the authors and publisher have made every effort to ensure there are no errors, inaccuracies, omissions, or inconsistencies herein, any slights or people, places, or organizations are unintentional.

*****

Cover illustration by Evan Jaroslow

Formatting by Debora Lewis arenapublishing.org

Other novels by Lauren B. Grossman

The Golden Peacock, a Rainee Allen mystery
Once in Every Generation

ISBN-13:978-1723304927
ISBN-10:1723304921

The Verona Exchange

A Rainee Allen mystery

Lauren B. Grossman

Bernard Jaroslow

This novel is dedicated to two people whose lives ended within nine months of each other.

First, our brother, Gary Jaroslow, whose departure created a chasm on this planet (appropriate as he was a marine geologist) and in our lives.

Second, our mother, Lillian Jaroslow, to whom we owe it all.

You both are deeply missed.

"A mother's love for her child is like nothing else in the world. It knows no law, no pity. It dares all things and crushes down remorselessly all that stands in its path."

~Agatha Christie, *The Hound of Death*

Prologue

December 1981

Evenings in late December always bustle in Verona. Excited children find it impossible to control their energy as they eagerly await the Christmas school break and their parents busily prepare for holiday festivities. Most households produce welcome holiday smells that passersby find difficult to resist. Baccalà, the customary salted fish, vermicelli, baked pasta, capon and turkey are prepared for festive suppers, accompanied by pastries that challenge even the strongest will. Lovely and peaceful Verona.

On a dark street corner, four commandos waited for a signal. Dressed in black from their balaclavas to their boots, they were too focused to notice the icy wind that swept along the street or the scents it carried.

None paid any attention to the holiday activity. They each had a job to do. They were brothers-in-arms, poised to shake up their native Italy and well trained to do it.

Other volunteers in the active cell of their homegrown terror organization had done the legwork and prepared every detail of the operation. Timing was paramount, as every previous successful operation had borne out.

Some of their earlier attempts at kidnapping had failed due to ineffective planning and poor operational timing. Failure had recently landed the founding leader of the nefarious organization in prison and nearly caused the disintegration of the entire faction. Several months afterward, new leadership bringing even bigger ideas sprouted from within its core. Buoyed by their successful kidnapping and murder of Italy's former Prime Minister, Aldo Moro, this new configuration of the Red Brigade members moved forward with this operation with newfound confidence and bravado.

Two men entered the front door and moved quickly to the back of the first-floor hallway. Their combat boots made hardly a sound as they traversed the ceramic tiles. Antonio led his partner down the darkened stairs to the dank, musty basement. Flashlights lit the way for the two. They moved easily among the maze of locked wooden storage units until they found the valves that controlled the main water lines. The old rusted valves squeaked when metal rubbed against metal as the men turned them off.

Both men moved quickly back up to the hallway and out the front door. They continued to the old, grey Daimler delivery truck waiting just around the corner beyond the reach of the white pool cast by the streetlight.

Inside the truck, Giuseppe and Carlo donned their field boots and thin leather gloves, then pocketed their freshly cut stocking masks and Beretta handguns. Despite their jangled nerves, both would be ready when they were needed.

The residents in the eighteen apartments noticed the lack of water immediately. Supper preparation, an almost sacred activity in Verona, halted.

Antonio slid the side door of the truck open as quietly as he could and stepped inside. "Bene?" Carlo asked as he finished his preparations.

"Tutto pronto," Antonio responded. "I give it five minutes before the first calls to Centro Veneto Servizi go out."

It was close. Seven minutes after the two men entered the truck, the first call went out. Promises were made by the official on the other end of the phone, but the apartment owners knew that those promises were not guarantees. Not at six o'clock on a cold winter's evening, just before supper.

The occupants of the truck waited. Timing would be everything. Too early and it would seem uncharacteristic of the service personnel to arrive so soon. Too late and the operation would be in danger of failure. Forty minutes was the agreed upon time. Time enough to move in, get to the right unit, do what they had to do and leave before any water service employees arrived.

At the forty minute mark, Antonio said, "Pronto. Let's move."

All four men left the truck, armed and ready for the mission. Antonio and Carlo entered first and made their way to the second floor. One minute later, Giuseppe and Luca joined them. A long hallway, wallpapered with a faded pastoral scene, led them to apartment 233.

Carlo knocked.

"Who's there?"

"Centro Veneto Servizi," Carlo responded.

He was rewarded by some shuffling footfalls and a man calling, "Un minuto." Seconds later the door opened and the nightmare began.

The four men charged into the apartment and made a beeline for the man inside. Each grabbed a flailing limb to immobilize the victim. Though he was not as young as they were, he was combat trained and gave them a difficult time.

Once the man was secured, Antonio applied a kerchief saturated with chloroform to his nose. In a few seconds the struggling man lost consciousness.

The Red Brigade had successfully kidnapped United States Brigadier General James L. Dozier.

One

March 2003

She used to love the sound of quiet. But that was when she lived alone on Marlborough Street in her Boston condominium.

Now that she was married and had a family, the sound of noise filled her up like the crescendo of a great symphony. Rainee felt gratitude and was content with her life.

Her mother-in-law was in the kitchen cooking. Her little daughter was watching the television and giggling. It was these sounds that uplifted her and brought appreciation and happiness. She no longer missed the quiet.

Late afternoon light had cast striped shadows from her shuttered windows. She noticed little rainbows reflected by the remaining droplets on the glass. It had been raining on and off all day.

Rainee turned the light on in her home office. *I have a little time before we eat, maybe I can get some writing done.*

She sat at her rolltop desk; one of the few pieces of furniture she had shipped from Boston to London after her wedding. It held a special place in her heart because her father had built it for her when her first novel was published.

She absentmindedly curled her brown hair through her long fingers as she waited for her computer to emerge from sleep mode. Rainee reread what was on her laptop screen and then poised her hands over the keyboard. The telephone's ring interrupted her thoughts. She answered it.

The man with the baritone voice on the other end of the phone said hesitantly, "Good morning. M-m-may I please speak with Rainee Allen."

"This is Rainee. It's really afternoon. Who is this?"

"Oh, God. I'm sorry, I forgot the time difference. Is this an inconvenient time? Do you want me to call back?"

"Who is this?"

"Yeah, right. Um... my name is Joshua. Joshua Greenberg." The end of his sentence lilted upward sounding almost like a question.

Rainee gasped. This was the phone call she had feared receiving for twenty-three years.

For a moment, she felt paralyzed. She cradled the phone close to her chest as her mind raced. She blinked away a tear and thought, *I must remember every single word.* Rainee wanted to be able to tell her husband, Martin, everything before the details faded like a dream.

The man on the phone was the child she had given up so many years before.

"My dad found your number. Hello? Are you still there?

Her heartbeat created a heavy percussive sound in her ears. She wondered if he could hear it over the phone.

"Oh yes. I'm still here. It's just... well, it's just... I guess I'm a little surprised. And a little nervous."

"I know. Fact is, I'm a little nervous myself. I probably hung up a dozen times before I dialed your number."

"Oh, sure. I can understand that."

"Yeah."

"Joshua... um... I'm not sure what to say. Uh, first of all, how are you?"

"I'm okay. Like I said, a bit nervous."

"Yeah. Sorry. I know this is awkward."

"Wasn't sure how you would take this. I mean...," he hesitated for just a moment, "...well, if you'd want to talk with me or not."

"Oh my God, yes. Yes, of course. I guess I just wasn't prepared or— well, I don't know what I mean."

Joshua's quiet laugh relaxed Rainee.

Her shoulders loosened, and she released a breath, unaware that she had been holding it. A moment passed.

"Joshua, I have to ask you something personal. I feel like it's the proverbial elephant in the room, but I need to ask it."

"Sure, go ahead."

"Did your father tell you the circumstances of your birth?"

"Yeah. Both my parents have been honest with me since I was little. They said if I ever wanted to get in touch with you, they would understand." He could hear Rainee quietly exhale. "Sorry, it took so long."

"You're sorry? I think it's me who needs to apologize." Rainee's voice cracked as she began to cry. She muffled the receiver, so he couldn't hear it.

"No. Please don't apologize. I didn't want to upset you."

He didn't want to upset me?

She cupped the receiver again and wiped her nose with a tissue. There was a long, awkward pause.

"Joshua, I'm glad you called. Really. Tell me about yourself. You must be... what... twenty-three now?"

"Yeah. I'm twenty-three. Almost twenty-four."

She knew that. Of course she knew. Even to the hour and minute he was born. You don't forget these things.

"Tell me more about yourself."

"I live in the D.C. area. I'm currently pursuing my PhD at S-CAR."

A PhD... my son, a doctor. Rainee felt pride welling up inside. "What is S-CAR?"

"Oh, that's the School for Conflict Analysis and Resolution. It's part of George Mason University."

"That's in Fairfax, Virginia, isn't it? Oh, so close to D.C. I've been to Washington. I loved it. You're lucky to be living in such an exciting area."

"Yeah, but S-CAR is in Arlington, just across the Potomac from the Mall."

"I hear that Arlington is a great place. A really happening place. But a PhD. That's fantastic. It really will be a great achievement. What will you do with it?"

"Probably teach, but there are many applications for conflict resolution. Mom calls it World Peace and— oh, I'm sorry."

"No. No, please. She *is* your mom. She raised you."

"Yeah, she did. Her name is Deborah and she's really great."

"I'm sure she is."

"Hey, I know this is awkward... for both of us. I was wondering if... well, I'm going to be in Europe in a couple of weeks, and I was hoping we could meet. That is if... if you want to, I mean."

A jolt fired through her body and a nervous knot tightened in her stomach.

"Yes. Yes, of course. I would really love to meet. Are you coming to London?"

"No, I'm actually attending a conference in Rome. My friend, Zack, is also going, but he has to leave right after the conference ends. I thought I would extend my trip a little and see Venice. I've never been there."

"Oh, Venice is wonderful! You will love it."

"Yeah, in high school I was in the plays *The Merchant of Venice* and *Romeo and Juliet*. I was actually Romeo! You know, forced to study Shakespeare. But truthfully, I enjoyed it. Would you like to meet in Venice? I mean, if you can get away."

"Joshua, I'd love to meet you in Venice. There's so much I have to say to you." Then she added, "You have a little sister. Did you know that?— oh, how could you know. She's five."

"Really? That's cool. What's her name?"

"Jana."

"Can you bring pictures of her?"

"Of course."

Rainee wrote down all the information about the conference and exchanged cell phone numbers. She asked him to call her when he got to Rome, and suggested he buy a throwaway phone there. His would probably not work in Europe.

Joshua said, "By the way, I read your books. I really liked them."

"I'm glad. Thanks, that means a lot to me."

"We'll talk soon. Can't wait. Bye."

Her hand was still trembling as she replaced the handset. Rainee sat a few minutes while she reflected on the conversation and collected her thoughts.

She had conflicted emotions. She was happy he called, but it stirred up old unresolved feelings. Feelings of anguish that arose from time to time throughout her life. She dreaded what he must think of her giving him away. Now that she was a mother, she could not fathom how she had come to that decision. As her own father reminded her on rare occasions, it was the right decision at the time. She wasn't ready to be a mother.

Rainee wanted to see the man he had grown into. The only picture she had of him was the hospital photo, where all infants looked like wrinkled old men. Now, with Joshua's call, she felt dismayed at having missed his childhood, his boyhood, his teenage years. Why had she not tried to get in touch with him first? Why did she wait for him to contact her?

The sound of giggles brought her back to her present reality. It was almost suppertime and Martin would be home soon. She walked into the den where their daughter, Jana, was watching television. She smiled at her precious girl, who lay on the floor resting on her elbows. She was staring up at the screen with pure, innocent glee.

Rainee said, "Sweetie, I thought I asked you to change out of your school uniform, so that it wouldn't wrinkle."

Jana was so engrossed in the television, she did not even react.

"Come keep Mummy and Nonna company while I make a salad."

Jana pouted. "I don't want to, Mummy. *Thomas and Friends* is on. I loooove this show."

"Okay but come into the kitchen as soon as it's over." Rainee felt overwhelmed by the phone call and wanted her little girl beside her.

Now that Jana was five years old, she was in school full-time. Her daughter had done a better job than Rainee, transitioning from the part-time pre-school years to full time. Previously, there had been time in the morning to write, but her afternoons were devoted to Jana. Now that school was most of the day, Rainee had all day to write, but when Jana came home, the five-year-old was often tired and would take much-needed naps. Rainee did not get to see her until after her nap and her favorite show was over.

She entered the kitchen. The pot roast was nearly cooked. Rainee lifted the lid and saw the juices bubbling. The aroma of the meat infused the air with warmth.

Her mother-in-law, Paloma, was in her wheelchair peeling potatoes; eyeglasses slipped to the end of her nose. *Should I tell her? No, I'll tell Martin first, then sit down and explain it all to her.*

Paloma looked over her shoulder. "Almost done. These will be delicious with tomorrow's chicken. I will roast them. Are we going to visit Aunt Jana in the nursing home tomorrow? Rainee? Rainee? Hello, Rainee, where are you?"

"Huh? Oh, yes, I was planning on it. I'll call John tomorrow and see if she's up for visitors." She opened the cabinet, removed four supper plates and placed them on the table.

Paloma wheeled herself from the table to the garbage bin to dump the potato skins. "That last visit was not a good one. She seemed very distant."

Paloma had long, elegant grey hair, which was almost always kept tied back in a braid, except when she cooked. Then, she would pin it into a bun atop her head. She finished with the messy chore, unpinned her hair, and allowed it to flow down her back. She then removed her favorite apron, which had her native Peruvian flag embroidered on it— a gift from her son.

"Yes. She was like when I first met her. I worry her Alzheimer's has advanced. It was as if she was looking for her brother all over again. I just wish she had more time with Ralf before he was sent away. She still calls him Max. Of course, I understand. That's how she knew her brother before they were separated. But I feel so helpless," Rainee said.

"Darling, we all do. But there is nothing we can do to stop the disease. You've been a good friend— I really should say, niece— to her."

Rainee took out the silverware and placed it beside each plate. "Still, to spend a lifetime of waiting for someone, only to lose him again."

Rainee shook her head. She realized the irony of that sentence. She had spent a lifetime— Joshua's lifetime— waiting for his call. She would do her best not lose him again.

"Yes, I feel the same way." Paloma's chin began to tremble, but she would not allow herself to cry. She missed her husband terribly.

Two

Paloma's multiple sclerosis had worsened when her husband stood trial. It nearly paralyzed her right side. Regardless of her discomfort and stress, she insisted on being at his trial every day. Ralf had been sent to prison for Nazi war crimes. He was scarred with the designation of crimes against humanity and sentenced to prison for the remainder of his life for killing hordes of people, principally Jews.

The terrible irony and burden that he bore was that he was, in fact, Jewish, who with his father, Henrik Lutken and his sister, Jana, fled Nazi Germany to Holland.

As a teenager he was put on a kindertransport from Amsterdam to Great Britain. His sister Jana's boat left one hour earlier.

Out of nowhere, the sky filled with German war planes and his boat was strafed, then bombed by the Luftwaffe on the North Sea. The explosion demolished the boat. Fire mutilated his body and flying metal struck his head. He was knocked overboard onto a piece of the ship's wreckage and lost consciousness. He awoke several times each day before his makeshift raft made landfall along the coast. Within hours, he was discovered by some young boys walking Holland's shoreline.

Eventually, he regained full consciousness and found that he was bandaged from head to toe in a German mobile hospital. His body eventually healed from the burns, but he suffered from total amnesia. Try as he might, he could not remember anything— most terrifying of all, who he was.

Because he spoke German, the Nazis assumed he was a soldier injured in the fighting. He accepted that presumption since he had no other explanation. When he was strong enough to fight, the soldiers gave him the name Ralf Wagner, handed him a rifle, and sent him to the front lines.

He was only sixteen, though he did not remember his own age. He was tough and smart. With no memory of his past, Ralf became emboldened by the power of being a soldier, and he became a good one. It did not take long for him to start believing the Nazi dogma and the propaganda against Jews and other non-Aryan races. It became all-consuming and he happily fulfilled his duty.

Ralf quickly climbed in rank. In due course, he was ordered to serve in a concentration camp where he began to wield his power over the Jewish prisoners.

When it became obvious that Germany was losing the war and the allies were approaching, he, like many other soldiers, fled the camp. Eventually, he made his way to South America. He found work in different cities and villages, always on the move, always on the run. Anonymity was his shield. In a remote village in Peru he saw Paloma, fell in love at first sight, and married her.

Years passed. During a local harvest festival, Ralf overheard a traveler singing a Yiddish lullaby to a child in his arms. The lullaby was titled, "The Golden Peacock." Without forethought, he hummed along, then started mouthing the foreign words. Memories flooded back. It was the same song his mother sang to him and his sister when they were young children. Somehow, he knew every strange word. Every musical note.

He was in shock. How could he know a Yiddish song? It took a few minutes to sink in. Out of the fog of distant memories, he was startled to remember his name was Max Lutken. And, he was Jewish!

He was bewildered. After all, he hated Jews, didn't he? He had even committed atrocities against them. But they were his people! He rationalized that he had carried out his duties in the name of his Fuehrer, Adolph Hitler. Shaken, confused, and ashamed, he made the decision to never tell his wife, Paloma. He would remain anonymous in his assumed identity of Ralf Wagner for the remainder of his life. He never told anyone.

Many years later, the family moved to London when their son, Martin, enrolled in medical school there. Ralf told his wife that they would have better opportunities in Europe. Better jobs. Better life quality. But in reality, he wanted to move closer to his roots and find out more about who he really was.

He knew he had a younger sister named Jana, with whom he had a very close relationship. Ralf had promised his father he would watch over her and protect her, and his guilt for not keeping his promise consumed him. If she was still alive, it would be important for him to reconnect with her.

The last thing he recalled of his sister was that she was on a Kindertransport leaving for England. It would stand to reason that if her boat was not attacked on the way, she might be somewhere in England. He lamented that Jana must have spent years wondering what had become of him.

Once established in London, Ralf secretly tried to find his sister. At one point, he hired a detective who came up empty. He searched the face of every woman approximately the age Jana would have been. He got a hold of old newspapers that might have given him a clue.

Nothing. After many years of searching, he gave up.

Author Rainee Allen came to London in search of the Holocaust survivor with whom she shared a birth date (with a thirty year difference). She found Jana Lutken Bowman in a nursing home. Sadly, Jana had Alzheimer's disease.

One day, Rainee witnessed Jana beside herself with fear when a young visiting doctor arrived. Rainee was curious why Dr. Martin Wagner's presence triggered Jana to relive the horrors of the Holocaust.

Her investigation led her to the doctor's father, Ralf. She could not know it then, but Ralf was Jana's long-lost brother.

After becoming aware that Rainee had stirred up unwanted attention, Ralf contacted an underground organization of Nazi sympathizers to rid himself of the woman who posed the threat of his exposure. He had no choice. If uncovered as a former Nazi, he would go to prison. Paloma would have no one to help her with her debilitating multiple sclerosis and it would be detrimental for his son's medical practice.

At the last minute, information surfaced that Jana was his sister. During a confrontation in a London park, he successfully stopped the two Nazi-sympathizer thugs he had sent to eliminate Rainee.

But not before a shot was fired, alerting two nearby Bobbies.

In the park, at that moment of seeing Jana for the first time since childhood, Ralf was aware that he was revealing who he was... a Nazi. He knew he would go to prison. Nevertheless, the years of searching for his sister, and hiding his true identity, were finally over.

During the long trial, Martin and Rainee spent a lot of time together. Eventually, they fell in love and married. She completed her second novel, which became a bestseller. They took in Paloma and moved Jana in with them as well. They hired full-time care for both in their London home. But after several months, Jana's Alzheimer's worsened. She began to wander out of the house. It was evident that she was looking for her brother Ralf. This became too dangerous for her and too difficult for them to handle. Sadly, they had to place her back in the nursing home.

After their first anniversary, happily Rainee became pregnant with a baby girl. There was no question about what her name would be.

Three

Paloma took a deep breath. "Poor Jana. All we can do is be there to support her and love her."

Rainee looked at her mother-in-law, and added sympathetically, "And Ralf."

Paloma managed a grateful smile and reached into her apron pocket. "Would you mind posting another letter for me?"

"Sure. To Ralf?"

"Of course. Who else? He wrote me he was ailing. The prison doctor said it was just a cold. But I worry that it could be pneumonia. He has even developed a persistent cough that just will not go away. He writes how dank those cells are. He has had it for two weeks now."

Rainee placed the last spoon. "Paloma, why didn't you tell Martin?"

"I had hoped it would be gone by now and I did not want to worry him. You know my son. He has enough on his mind, taking care of all of us *and* his patients."

"We'll tell him when he gets home. He'll want to go and examine Ralf himself." The two women finished setting the table together.

Little Jana came into the kitchen holding her stuffed giraffe.

"Mummy, can I have a biscuit?"

Rainee corrected her. "*May* I have a biscuit, *please*."

"May I, Mummy? Pleaaaaase?"

"No, Jana. It's almost suppertime. But you can have one for dessert."

Jana pouted. That pout melted Rainee's heart, but she stayed firm. "Sweetie, give me a big hug."

Her daughter ran into her arms and squeezed her tightly. Then she ran to Paloma and did the same. Then she ran to sit at the table and pretended to feed her giraffe.

Rainee chuckled. *That girl is always running. What energy!*

The front door opened and closed, and moments later Martin stood by the kitchen door. He put his index finger to his lips to intend a shush. Martin loved to watch Jana while she was busy playing.

Rainee loved that he did this every evening. It gave her moment to appraise this devoted man with whom she fell in love. He favored his mother with dark eyes and tanned complexion. His hair had receded and grayed even more than when she had first met him. But given all he and Paloma had gone through with Ralf's trial, and the news it generated, it was understandable. He was grateful that most of his patients had not left his practice. Those that did, slowly migrated back to him.

What she loved most about his appearance was not his six foot height, nor his large arms that, when he enveloped her with them, made her feel protected. Or that the whitest tooth in his mouth was still a baby tooth. Not even his throw-your-head-back laugh. No, it was his amused smile. When he was amused, like now, or when they played games, it was like he was trying to keep his lips tight while withholding a smile— as if he had a secret. And this produced a sweet and slightly pursed smile.

At last Martin said, "Well, here are my girls."

Jana squealed with delight, jumped out of her chair and into his arms. Then in the same order he followed every night, he kissed Jana, Rainee, and then his mother.

"What did you bring me, Daddy?"

"Hmm. Well, let me see." Martin sat on a kitchen chair with Jana on his lap. He fished around in his shirt pocket and pulled out a blue, plastic magnifying glass. It never mattered what he brought home— it could be just a ball of thread— as long as he had something new to give her.

"What is it, Daddy?"

"Look through it, and see how big small things become."

Jana jumped off his lap and ran around the kitchen looking through her new toy.

"How was work, Honey?"

"It was interesting, to say the very least."

Both women said in unison, "Why?"

"I've been asked to speak at a convention about recent advances in research for MS. A speaker must have dropped out. It would mean rearranging my schedule, and I really hate to do that to my patients. I might pass on the invitation."

"When is it?" Rainee was thinking about her trip to Venice.

"Next month. We'll see. We'll talk about it. You know I hate being away from my girls."

Paloma said, "Yes, but Martin, if it helps advance knowledge about multiple sclerosis—"

"I know, Mother. And I agree. We'll see. I just got the invitation today."

Thankfully, Paloma's multiple sclerosis was now stable. She had become adept at using a wheelchair to get around. To Rainee's amusement, she always had a purse tucked to her side, even in the house.

From the moment they had met, Rainee felt Paloma was a gentlewoman, with a good heart and polished manners. Paloma never complained about her MS, but did about being a burden to her family. Both Martin and Rainee assured her that she was not a burden and was welcome to live with them for as long as she could tolerate them.

During supper and to the amusement of the adults, little Jana chatted nonstop. Rainee had to remind her to stop talking while she chewed her food. She would stop, swallow, and then begin talking again.

Martin, Rainee and Paloma lovingly laughed at the little girl with the blonde Shirley Temple curls. Martin asked, "Now, who does she take after?"

"You mean the curly blonde hair? Not my family," Rainee said.

"I'm thinking more of the non-stop chatting." Martin pointed his finger at his wife, knowing the answer.

Rainee admitted, "Guilty as charged."

Even little Jana laughed.

After Jana fell asleep for the night, and in the privacy of their bedroom, Rainee told Martin about her phone call from Joshua.

Martin had known about her history and her decision to give up a child. He admired her for being able to have made that tough decision at the youthful age of twenty-one.

She was unmarried and had become pregnant by her close friend, Ricky. She was neither mature enough nor prepared to have a child. She wanted a career and to experience life.

Ricky had known it would take a lot of convincing, but he wore her down. Rainee acquiesced only because Ricky said that he would raise the child himself. Ricky named the baby Joshua and moved with him to California. Rainee never heard from her best friend again.

Besides her family, the only other person who knew of the arrangement was her best friend, Shelley. Though it was Rainee's resolute decision to give up the child, it left an emptiness in her. She buried any feelings of regret deep in the recesses of her heart and never spoke of it. Yet, when Rainee watched mothers with their children, she would often feel a slight pang of remorse. It was not until she gave birth to Jana that the hole felt somewhat filled. Her thoughts of what became of Ricky and Joshua began to slowly lessen, thanks to the wonder, and busy energy, of her beautiful little girl.

Martin smiled at her and said, "Rain, you knew that someday you might find yourself in this position."

"Yes, but I still wasn't prepared for the phone call. I was actually trembling."

The gentle patter of raindrops hitting their bedroom window made Rainee shake her head. "London weather. Will I ever get used to it?"

Martin laughed. "My love, you would think after seven years... ."

He led her to their chaise lounge, gently sat her down, and placed a plush cushion behind her back. He straddled the chair, put his arms around his wife's shoulders and pulled her close. "I think this is good. It will bring closure for you. You're doing the right thing. Joshua wants to meet his biological mother. And you know you're curious. You want to meet him, too."

"Of course, I do. He's going to call when he gets to Rome. We'll meet in Venice. Boy, I never thought I'd be this nervous."

"It's understandable."

"Thanks for being so accepting, Honey."

Martin tightened his arms. "It'll be a nice break from all you do around here... taking care of my mother and my aunt and our child. Who knows, maybe you'll find another plot for your next book in Venice."

She smiled. "Nope. Not bringing my laptop this time. I don't want anything to distract from my time with Joshua."

"How did I get so lucky? So now Jana has a big brother." He grinned and started kissing her neck. "What do you say we give her a little brother?"

Rainee put her arms around Martin.

He stood, picked her up in his strong arms, and carried her to their bed.

She said, "Darling, we've talked about this before. At my age it's not a great idea. Don't get me wrong. You know I love the idea, but even if I got pregnant tonight, I would be... what?... a month away from turning forty-eight when the baby's born."

"Still young, brilliant, strong, and beautiful. Not to mention ravishing." He kissed her on the lips.

Rainee gently stopped him. "Martin, remember what the doctor said after I gave birth to Jana at forty-two? It was a touch-and-go delivery. Thank God, she is perfect. Then the miscarriage a year later. That was awful. We can't take the chance again. I won't go through that again."

Martin cupped her face in his hands, then kissed her eyelids. "Rainee, my love, all I need is you and Jana. You two are my life."

He kissed her neck again with soft kisses and her body responded. She pulled him closer and kissed his lips. All her thoughts of the past and the future that had cluttered her mind fell away as they made love.

The raindrops drummed louder against the window pane as the light London rainfall turned into a storm.

Four

They arrived on a chilly April morning at Leonardo da Vinci International, one of Europe's busiest airports. Guards with their ubiquitous machine guns were a not-so-subtle reminder of the dangerous days of leftist organizations such as the Baader-Meinhof group, Rote Armee Fraktion, the Italian Brigate Rosse, and others who started a decades-long period of Euro-terrorism. Those groups' very existence was the result of their disdain for western capitalism and right-leaning governments. Unfortunately, the route they took to try to achieve their dreams involved aggression and brute force. The period was hard. The tactics deadly.

Joshua and his buddy, Zachary Abee, were visiting Rome for the first time. Though tired, the two young men were wide-eyed.

Zack had become Joshua's friend on his first day at GMU. Over the years they became best friends and were almost inseparable. The result of their incessant studying was outstanding grades. The friends received the top grades in the program. It was generally known they had the best chance to fill the relatively few coveted positions in Conflict Resolution.

When they first read a flyer about the global conflict resolution conference in Italy, their excitement was palpable. Each had always wanted to visit Europe, and Italy in particular. Immediately, they carried out extensive research about Rome and made plans. They simply had to go. Then, fortuitously, Professor Esposito asked Joshua to deliver his paper with him, and here they were.

They planned their arrival so they could enjoy a long weekend in Rome before the meeting would start. Rome had always held an historical fascination for both of them, but those ancient sites would have to wait. After more than ten hours of travel, a shower, shave, and a fresh set of clothes took precedence over anything fun or educational.

The taxi they took from Fumicino was dirty, the floor mats were sticky, and their seat belts did not retract, but neither of the guys cared. They tried to talk with the driver, but he had little command of English, so after a few attempts, they stopped asking him questions.

After what seemed to be a long and circuitous route, the driver dropped them at the Hotel Condotti near the famous Spanish Steps, which were always crowded with tourists and local teenagers. The driver charged an amount they thought was excessive, but what could they do?

As they entered the hotel they looked at each other and smiled. Each took a deep breath. Italy. They were finally here.

The hotel was conveniently located in the heart of Rome. It was surrounded by restaurants, bars, shops and many of Rome's tourist attractions.

On this trip, however, Joshua's time would be limited. He would only be able to devote three days to sightseeing at the beginning of his trip, four days at the conference, and two days to get to know Rainee.

Twenty-three years without ever knowing– or even meeting– my birth mother, he thought. *I'm excited and nervous. I need to buy one of those pay-by-time phones and let her know I'm here. I did promise.* He thought back to that telephone conversation. The first one he ever had with his biological mother.

His emotions were conflicted after he said goodbye to her on the phone. On one hand, he was very happy to connect with his biological mother, if only through the phone. On the other hand, she did leave him with his father just after he was born. Although his father had explained Rainee's reservations about raising a child, it was always something that bothered him. *Who could do that to their own baby? How different would my life have been if I had grown up with her?*

In a few days, he would be face-to-face with her, and he wondered what his emotions would be like. What his first words would be. Would she cry? Would he cry?

But there would be time to think about meeting her later. His thoughts turned to the present.

Joshua looked forward to meeting up with his respected professor and mentor, Dr. Antonio Esposito, whose presentation he was sharing at the conference.

Dr. Esposito had seen a spark of something in Joshua Greenberg during his first week at George Mason University. A wide-eyed and scared student who wanted to change the world. Since that day five years before, the young man had morphed into an intelligent and thoughtful theorist, well-trained in policy and program development, cultural analysis and regional history. It was this spark that led the professor to start a long-term, mentor-student relationship with him, one that set Joshua on a path of excellence and commitment. The fruits of their collaboration would soon be shared with hundreds of their colleagues from around the world.

The professor was to meet both of them in the lobby of their hotel on Monday morning at six-thirty for breakfast before they left for the conference.

Joshua's mind wandered to the day just a couple of months before, when the professor asked him to share the podium with him in Italy.

The sound of the bell was cheered by the class.

The professor said, "Okay, everyone. Make sure you read chapters twelve through fourteen in the *International Conflict*

Resolution after the Cold War textbook. And dig deep, because a fair amount of next week's exam will include information from those chapters." He paused and looked about the lecture hall. "Mr. Colton, I'm still waiting for your assignment. And Mr. Greenberg, don't leave immediately. I'd like to speak with you."

The class adjourned and the students filed out the door.

A worried Joshua Greenberg remained. *Did I mess something up?* He approached the desk. "Yes sir, Professor. You need me for anything?"

"I do, Joshua. Do you have a few minutes?" But before Joshua had a chance to respond, he said, "Good. Walk with me."

"Of course, Professor. What's up?"

"I think I have a unique opportunity for you. Come. Let's go. I don't want to be late. I'm meeting Professor Cunningham for lunch. She doesn't like tardiness."

The two walked across a busy North Fairfax Drive and away from the campus buildings.

"Joshua, you must know that I think highly of you. You have shown a profound interest in my classes, and of course, your grades reflect that interest. For that reason, I would like to offer you a chance to do something special.

As you know, the article that you helped me write last year was published. Remember 'Inclusive Middle Eastern Conflict Resolution Practices in the 21st Century'?"

Joshua nodded. "Of course."

"The paper seems to have touched off a small debate of sorts in some of the schools of our European colleagues. So much so that I have been invited to defend its premise in the annual conference of the International Association of Ethno-Religious Mediation. They want me to present the paper at their conference in Rome."

"Wow, Professor, that's great news! I'm excited for you!"

"Thank you, Joshua, but I didn't tell you about this for praise. I'm telling you because I want you to present with me at the meeting this Spring. The school will cover all your expenses. Would you be interested?"

"Interested? Of course! That is so awesome! Wow! You want me to present with you? What about Zack Abee or Liz Maxwell or Bob Leader? They're great students too."

"That's true, but frankly, you deserve the honor after all the work you did to help me put the article together. It might have taken me an additional several months had you not spent so much of your time researching information for me. No, you deserve this. I have given a lot of thought to it. My co-presenter must be you."

"Cool! Thank you so much, Professor. What an honor. Sure, I'd be honored to present with you. I've never even been to Rome!"

"Really? That's surprising, given your father's, uh... status. I would have thought you would have been there for a family vacation or something."

"Nope. We have been to Europe, but not to Italy. I am looking forward to this! Thank you so much. I hope I'll make you proud and not regret asking me!"

"I have no doubt you will. I had better get a move on. Mary Ann won't like it if I'm late."

With that, the two men shook hands and parted ways.

Joshua was excited. He thought, *I've got to call Mom and Dad. They'll be so proud! Oh, man, what about Zack? He'll be heartbroken. He wanted to go to the Rome conference. I've got to call him.*

Joshua took out his cell phone and dialed his friend.

"Hello," Zack answered in a sleepy voice at the other end.

"Zack, it's me. Josh. Guess what? Professor Esposito asked me to go and present with him at that conference we were checking out!"

"Oh my God! No way! Hey, congratulations! You deserve it, dude. I'm so glad you get to go, even though you know I'm the one who's dying to see Rome!" He laughed.

"I know. I know. I feel kind'a bad about that. Would you still be willing to come? Do you think your dad would pay for you? What do you think? I bet we could wrangle you a badge for the conference. You could help us set up. That'll make the conference free for you. I'm sure the professor would help with that. What do you think? It would be awesome! You and me in Rome like we planned."

"That does sound awesome, Josh. Let me work on it and I'll let you know. I think my dad would want me to go, but it's just that he may not have the funds right now."

"Yeah, I get it. Hey, what if I helped you out with at least some of it? If your dad could come up with half, I would be willing to pay the rest. It's worth it for me to have you there. We'd have a blast! What do you say?"

"God, that sounds amazing. Let me get back to you. Wow! Rome! How cool!"

Joshua thought, *I'm so glad he wants to come with me. He'll be there to support me for sure, and we get to have some fun in Rome together too!*

Joshua came from wealth, but Zack did not. Zack was on scholarships at the school since he started, and he continued getting grants in his postgraduate years. He was an excellent student. Better than Joshua. Zack seemed to immediately understand and remember everything with barely any studying.

That was not the case with Joshua. He had to spend hours each night reading and analyzing, and it didn't always stick. In fact, though his grades were good, he felt a little guilty about being the one who was originally picked to help research the paper with the professor. It didn't make sense to him because he knew in his heart that Zack was the better choice. Zack's grades were definitely better, and delivering presentations seemed to be natural to him.

As they waited in line to check in to the hotel, Joshua thought about his lecture with Dr. Esposito. *Are my slides in the right order? Did I forget anything? I can't fail. It would really let the professor down.*

What am I doing? I went over the slides a hundred times! They're in the right order. The professor and I worked on the presentation together and he gave it the green light. What am I worried about?

Besides, he could worry later. The weekend belonged to Rome.

Tired, but excited, they entered their hotel room and looked around. It was nice, but not overly fancy. The long pillows spanned the width of the beds, making up for their narrowness. The blue sofa was hard, but comfortable enough. They would not be spending much time on it anyway. The bathroom was as small as possible. It did have a window that offered a clear view, unfortunately of another guest room, just feet away.

Both of the young men unpacked and hung their clothes. Joshua had brought two of his best and most expensive suits for the conference, and also packed his ever-present blue blazer. He wore it to class, to parties, on dates and even to the grocery store. He rarely went anywhere without it. Growing up privileged meant dressing well for certain occasions, and he would make discovering Rome one of those.

He attempted to shake out the wrinkles of his button-down shirts and hung them in the tiny closet on the wooden hangers. He used two of the hangers to hang his suits on the shower curtain rod to steam later that evening. Underwear, socks and sleeping shirts were unceremoniously tossed into one of the two drawers in the dresser.

Zack could not have been more different. His jeans and requisite rock and roll t-shirts defined his true persona—young, hip and casual. He claimed a tiny fraction of the closet for the one brown suit and matching tie he planned to wear throughout the conference. The packing wrinkles weren't of much concern. A different colored shirt each day would help to make his appearance look a little different.

When they finished unpacking, Joshua sat down on the sofa and Zack plopped onto the bed. After a few minutes of conversation, Joshua went into the bathroom to wash up and change. He glanced into the mirror and saw a very tired face. His hair was mussed and he needed to shave, but there would be plenty of time for that later. Now it was time for Rome.

Both threw on a fresh t-shirt and some jeans. Joshua grabbed his blazer. They pocketed their wallets and took the large skeleton keys down the steps to the lobby where they dropped them off and asked for directions to a store where they could purchase cell phones.

Rainee answered after the third ring. "Hello."

"Hi. It's Joshua."

"Joshua! Hello! It's so good to hear your voice. Are you in Rome?"

"I am," he replied. "I'm calling you from one of those cheap phones you asked me to buy. It seems to work fine. Let me give you the phone number." He could hear her scrambling to find a pen. Finally he gave her the new number.

"What time did you get in? Was it a good flight? Did you check into your hotel? Is your room all right?"

Joshua chuckled. "Don't worry. Everything's fine. The flight was long and uneventful. I slept through most of it. I'm all set with my hotel. I even brushed my teeth when I arrived!"

Rainee covered her embarrassment with laughter. "Oh. I'm sorry, Joshua. I guess I'm just excited for you. Oh, and you should know this about me: I talk a lot when I'm nervous."

He smiled. "It's okay, Rainee. I understand."

She wasn't sure why hearing him call her Rainee unsettled her, but it did.

I guess I deserve it. And besides, what else should he call me? Mom? I suppose that might be just as awkward.

She said, "You know, I researched this conference on the Internet. Your picture and bio, along with Dr. Esposito's, was on the conference website." She had stared at her son's face for a long time, burning his image into her brain. "Very exciting! When will you be finished with your conference? We need to determine a time to meet."

"I should be finished with my commitments by Friday around noon. Then I'll take the train to Venice. You'll need to pick the hotel. I've never been there before, and I have no idea where anything is."

"My husband has arranged a room for you at my hotel. You'll love it. It's so... old-world Venice!" She gave him the name of the hotel and the street address.

"Would you call me sometime after your presentation Thursday? I want to hear how it went. Then, call me as soon as you arrive at the Venice train station."

"Sounds great, Rainee. See you then. Ciao."

"Ciao," she responded with a slight wince after hearing him say her name again.

The temperature was a bit cool, but the skies were an azure blue, with scattered puffy white cumulus clouds. Joshua and Zack were anxious to start experiencing Rome.

Where to first? thought Joshua.

He talked with Zack and they consulted the tourist map the hotel clerk had given them. They chose the Vatican museums for their first stop. Before they caught a taxi, they agreed that they would walk down the Spanish Steps, since it was so close to the hotel.

As they saw when they arrived, the steps were crowded by dozens of people. Some just sat and talked, some threw Frisbees, and some quietly read their books despite the tumult that surrounded them.

Once they reached the bottom, they saw a plaque on a building commemorating the place where the English author John Keats lived and died. Zack took his first picture in Rome as an official tourist. They hailed a taxi.

The short journey to the Vatican was wonderful in and of itself. The style of the buildings fascinated the young men, both of whom had an interest in architectural design. Joshua, who grew up traveling the world with his parents, found himself comparing the different styles of buildings with those he was more familiar with throughout western Europe, while Zack marveled at the unique design characteristics of the structures. They saw wonderful examples of Romanesque, Gothic, Renaissance and Baroque-styled buildings. They marveled that even though the buildings themselves were only several hundred years old, some of their styles were created almost three-thousand years ago.

Then, as the taxi made a right turn, they saw the Colosseum. The magnificent structure was built in approximately 80 A.D.

"Zack. Look! Oh my God. There it is. The Colosseum! Can you believe it? It's over nineteen hundred years old and it's still standing. Well, mostly. I read that the locals stole a lot of its stone blocks, and usually in the dead of night, to use for the construction of their homes."

Zack was silent. Just shaking his head like he really could not believe it.

"Supposedly, it took over sixty thousand slaves to build it. And get this: over four hundred thousand people and over one million animals died inside! Man, I can't wait to check it out."

Zack replied, "I wonder if they had guys walking around serving hot dogs and beer during those events? Get your red-hot chili dogs here!" They both laughed.

This time the taxi driver made conversation and the discussion centered around *Dallas*, his favorite television show. He wanted their opinions on whether they thought J.R. Ewing and Sue Ellen should remarry. Joshua and Zack looked at each other and shrugged.

Still talking about *Dallas*, the taxi driver maneuvered his way to the Vatican, using back streets. Before long, the taxi came to a halt, and the two friends stepped out onto the hallowed grounds.

The experience was wonderful, and both were overwhelmed with the history of the Vatican and its museums. They seemed to not be able to get enough of the art. Predictably, as soon as they entered the museum area, they both made a beeline for the Sistine Chapel to bathe in the frescos of Michelangelo— especially the scene entitled, *The Creation of Adam*, where the finger of God barely touches that of Adam.

They both stared upwards for several minutes. Zack broke the silence. "Man, it's hard to believe Michelangelo did all of this while lying on his back."

"Yeah, I couldn't even trace it sitting comfortably at a desk," Joshua said with a grin.

The works of Da Vinci, Titian, Raphael, and other masters also touched them in a way they had not expected. The history. The beauty. They stayed for several hours, ate lunch at a nearby trattoria and planned out their next site.

It was not long before they were standing in front of the Trevi Fountain, the largest Baroque fountain in the city and one of the most dramatic and beautiful in the world. One thing Zack noticed as he got close to it was the very large number of coins in the fountain.

Joshua knew it well, because *Three Coins in a Fountain* was one of Deborah's favorite movies. Legend had it that if tourists threw coins into the water, they would have good luck and were assured future visits to Rome.

Joshua reached into his pocket to find some coins but came up empty. He had converted his U.S. currency into Euros but had left the coins on a table in his room at the hotel.

"How about you, Zack? Do you have any change?"

"Nope, sorry. Only paper money, and I don't think I should throw that in."

Oh well, Joshua thought, *I don't have to throw any in now. I know I'll be back.* "You know, I think we already have good luck, Zack. I doubt we'll need any more."

There were still a couple of hours of daylight left and they decided they would see everything they could in the three days they had free. They consulted their Rome tourist city map. It had lots of recommendations, but they zeroed in on something: the Pantheon. The map said it was one of the oldest and best-preserved structures in Italy, just shy of two thousand years old. "Okay, let's grab a taxi."

"Well, what did you read about this, Mr. History Scholar?" Zack asked Joshua.

"Funny you should mention it! I did read about it! It was a temple to the gods when it was first built, and to this day they don't even know what it was made out of! Isn't that weird? It's some sort of concrete-like material that somehow was strong enough to last all this time. Even through all of the storms and lightning strikes."

"Not to mention wars."

Joshua nodded.

"Wow. Amazing," replied Zack. "Anyone famous buried in it?"

"Yeah, there is. Actually, Raphael, whose art we just saw in the Vatican Museum, is buried there, along with some kings whose names I don't know."

They enjoyed their time in the cylindrical interior.

The weather was turning cold. Joshua noticed that Zack was shivering and suggested they go back to the hotel to grab some warmer clothes. Growing increasingly tired, they figured an early first night would leave a couple of evenings for some Roman night life. They would find a nice restaurant to cap off their first day in Rome.

Sunday and Monday were equally fun and satisfying for the two students.

It was a beautiful Sunday morning that started with a return to the Vatican to watch Pope John Paul II deliver his blessing to the masses from his window in St. Peter's Basilica. Both Joshua and Zack were Jewish, but they wanted to witness the event and see the world figure live. They did and it was fun, but they did not dawdle. There was lots more to see.

Circus Maximus was the next item on Joshua's must-see list. He had watched the movie *Ben Hur* with his father years before and wanted to see where the chariot races actually took place in ancient Rome. He even challenged Zack to a foot race around the track.

Zack accepted happily, but much to their dismay, there was no more track. Just a green, grass-covered field. That did not stop them, though. They made it around barely one quarter of what had once been the track before collapsing on the ground and laughing together.

They were giddy, but each felt a real sense of history where the lay. Around this track two thousand years ago, slaves in a small chariot did their utmost to steer their four horses around a track at breakneck speeds, sometimes running other chariot drivers off the track and into the wall. Whatever it took to come in first, at whatever the cost and in the name of freedom.

They spent the rest of their last two sightseeing days visiting other historical sites around Rome. The Catacombs, the Roman Forum, and they even walked a little on the Appian Way.

Their nights were spent in clubs drinking and dancing. They covered a lot in a short time and it was all worth it. The meetings would start in the morning, so they reluctantly returned to their hotel and collapsed onto their beds.

Five

On the plane to Venice, Rainee went over various scenarios in her mind. Meeting her son. Explaining her version of what had transpired twenty-three years ago. Why she gave him up. She now knew Ricky had explained it to him, but she wanted Joshua to hear her version.

Her mind wandered to the last time she visited Venice. It was their honeymoon. Martin had picked a hotel close to the Piazza San Marco because it was a central location. The travel agent advised them that you can never get lost in Venice because signs always pointed the way to that plaza. The hotel was very romantic. Martin had seen to that.

Familiar with Venice, he arranged many of the events. One was a private and romantic gondola ride with an Italian tenor on board who sang love songs to the newlyweds. Others included day trips to the different islands of Venice. There was Murano, famous for their glass, where Rainee picked out a beautiful chandelier for their dining room. Then a wonderful day was spent on the colorful and picturesque island of Burano, famous for its lace, where Rainee purchased magnificent handmade scarves for Paloma and Jana.

Her mind flipped back to the real reason for this trip. Meeting Joshua. She wondered what would he think of her? Her nervousness returned, and she ordered a vodka tonic.

The patchwork appearance of the earth appeared beneath the clouds as the plane began its descent into Marco Polo Airport.

She gulped down the last few drops of her drink and placed her seat and tray table into the upright position.

After she retrieved her luggage, Rainee took a water taxi to the central island of Venice. The driver steered slowly down the narrow canal to the steps of her hotel.

The hotel Ai Cicerone was known for its tall ceilings, marbled hallways, and quiet charm. It had once been an aristocratic Venetian palace, and was located in the center of the city, between Rialto and Piazza San Marco.

Rainee noted that Venetians were polite, but never in a hurry. The hotel clerk nodded when she approached the desk but did not stop his typing.

After a few minutes of gazing at the balding spot on the top of his head, Rainee cleared her throat to get his attention.

He looked at her quizzically, then rose to address her. "Si, Signora, may I help you?"

"Yes. I have a reservation under Rainee Allen." She had kept her maiden name because of her recognition as an author and to help further promote her in her profession. Plus, by the time she married, she had been Rainee Allen for forty-two years. Martin understood and had no objection.

"Ah, si!" He had her sign forms, show identification, handed her the room key, and then rang for a bellhop to help with the luggage.

She smiled. She could never get used to the oversized key chains older European hotels often gave their guests to encourage them to turn them in when they left the hotel.

The luxurious suite consisted of a large living area furnished with fine furniture and beautiful wooden flooring. The room was decorated in elegant 18th century Venetian style, with antique textiles on the walls. Even the bedroom was furnished with antique furniture and overlooked the quiet canal. Somewhat incongruous with all the opulence was an Internet connection, a state-of-the-art flat screen TV, and Wi-Fi. Rainee laughed at how out-of-place these 21st century items appeared.

She tipped the bellhop, then opened the doors to the balcony to let in the air. She stepped out to admire the view. Fortunately, her suite was on the fourth floor, so the often fetid smell of Venice's canals did not reach her nose.

Martin arranged the hotel stay. He understood her apprehension and anxiety of the upcoming meeting and wanted her to relax and enjoy herself. She should have guessed he would pick out something so lovely. She whispered, "Thank you, my love."

She kicked off her heels, then ran the bath water. Fresh rose-scented potpourri sat on the vanity, so Rainee sprinkled some into the water.

She caught her image in the Baroque-styled bathroom mirror and leaned in to search for new wrinkles.

Damn, where does the time go? When we met seven years ago, did these crevasses even exist? Laugh lines. Ha! Worry lines are more like it. And here's another silver hair. She pulled it out.

Turning sideways, Rainee scrutinized her figure.

At least I was able to lose all that weight after Jana was born. I may weigh the same as when we got married, but it has all... kind of shifted.

She rolled her eyes, and admonished her reflection, "Knock it off, girl. He loves you the way you are."

Rainee tested the bath water and stepped cautiously into the steaming tub. She wanted to feel and look good when she met her son the next day.

She chose a small outdoor table in busy Piazza San Marco and sipped a cappuccino, while she watched the tourists take selfies with outstretched arms. Even though she had been there a couple of times before, she never got used to the sheer number of pigeons, lured by tourists all too happy to feed them. Rainee loved that the plaza had not changed as the social center for Venetians for the last eight-hundred years.

The day was lovely. The perfect temperature accompanied a cloudless sky. The Campanile's clock tower bells rang out loudly and beautifully. A sound Rainee had first heard at the very moment when she and Martin shared a kiss. After that kiss, it became their own tradition to kiss when they heard it ring out. She stared at the stunning Basilica San Marco, with its Byzantine mosaics, part of the magnificent Doge's Palace. *It's a wonder these buildings are still standing and have stayed so beautiful*, she thought.

She appreciated how Venice was a floating masterpiece, both extraordinary and romantic. The residents always seemed to dress well and parade in the streets and along the canals all day and night. Whether going to or returning from work or dining al fresco in the evening, there were always crowds coming and going.

"*Scusami. Hai tempo, bella signora.*"

Rainee turned to see two young men asking her for the time. They were about Joshua's age, and had been drinking. She glanced at her watch and told them.

Rainee smiled, remembering Joshua's own previous late-night call from Rome.

He had been noticeably intoxicated, slurring some of his words, while he celebrated with a friend and the man he called his mentor.

"The presentation went per-fect-ly," he said, enunciating each syllable. "Must've been three hundred people in the audience."

"That's impressive, Joshua. Were you nervous?"

"Well, yeah, at first. But after a while, I forgot about the people and just talked. I hardly used my cue cards." Then he either giggled or burped. Rainee was not sure which.

"I would have loved to have been there. Was it videoed?"

"Yep. The content is part of my doctoral thesis. Y'know, Rainee, I think I knocked this one outta the ballpark."

"Really?" She could tell by his voice that he had a big smile on his face.

"Oops. I didn't mean to brag. Not professional. Sorry."

"God no, you have every right to brag. I hope I get to watch that video someday. Where are you now? It sounds noisy."

"Yeah, we're in a bar. We're celebratin'. Just my professor, Zack and me."

"Who is Zack?"

The phone was ripped out of Joshua's hands. "Hi, Ms. Allen. This is Zachary Abee. I'm a friend of the J-man here. Just wanna say he really did a grrrreat job. You would'a been very proud."

Rainee laughed, "Well, Zachary, I'm glad he had you there to support him. I would love to meet you some day."

"Yeah, me too. I mean, me too to meet you." He giggled.

Rainee heard Joshua telling Zachary to hand him back his phone.

"Excuse the inter—" There was the sound of a hiccup, "—ruption. That's Zack, my best friend, also from GMU. Zack Abee. I call him, Zachary Daquiri. So we're all celebratin'. Celebratin' together. The three of us. In a bar in Rome. Not with Daquiris, though."

Rainee smiled at the merriment in his voice.

Joshua said, "Can I call you tomorrow? I mean, when I get to Venice. It's a li'l hard to hear in this place. Plus, I gotta get back to celebratin'."

"Absolutely. Go and enjoy. Looking forward to seeing you tomorrow. And congratulations!"

"Thanks a mill—." He hung up.

She laughed, remembering what it was like to be young and on your own. Her mind traveled back to her early days with Ricky.

Ricky... they had vowed to be best friends forever. Everyone said that platonic relationships did not work, but they proved them wrong. He was like a brother to her.

They met in the school library in seventh grade. The mystery stacks. Ricky came around the corner, his face close to the books, head turned sideways as he tried to read the titles on the books' spines. He almost tripped over Rainee, who was sitting cross-legged with a tall pile of books.

She looked up. "Hey, watch it."

He looked down. "Oops, sorry. You're sitting right under a book I want. I can't reach it."

"I'll move."

She knew him by his face. Everyone at that school knew each other by face, if not by name. It was a small junior high school.

He apologized again. "Sorry about that. Y'know, it's just that I haven't read this one yet, and I really, really want to."

Rainee looked up. "I read it already. The kid's step-brother killed the girl." She grinned.

"Hey, thanks a lot."

"Now we're even."

"Sure, okay. We're even." He eyed the stack of books beside her. "Looks like you are really into mysteries."

"Yep." She picked one up and passed it up to him. "Here, you might like this one."

"I don't want to take one you're thinking of reading."

"It's okay. I already eliminated it."

"Eliminated it? Like with a process of elimination?" He sat down across from her.

"Yep. Doesn't everyone have a process?"

"I dunno, do they?"

"I do. First, I take all these down. But since you can only check out three, I use deductive reasoning to eliminate the other books. Just like all great sleuths do."

He nodded as if he understood, which he did not.

"I read the synopsis on the back, and if it's interesting I put it in that pile." She pointed. "But if it can wait, like the one I handed you, it goes in that pile." She pointed again. "Then, when I get down to three, I weigh them with my hands. Two light, one heavy. Then I check them out."

Ricky laughed and it turned into a snort. That made Rainee laugh.

Ricky was what the kids called a nerd. He was excited about computers and confided in Rainee that one day he would build his own computer. He had big dreams. He told her excitedly that Atari had just released Pong, the first commercial video game. Someday, he said, he was going to buy the company. Then he moved on to the programming language FORTRAN 66. It had just been created and he was going to learn it.

Rainee yawned while he talked excitedly. Computer talk whizzed right over her head. She wondered what this guy was talking about.

But she liked him. He was different, and she was different too. Rainee was a loner. She did not really fit in with any of the cliques at school, so she mostly stayed to herself. She would rather be reading books than hanging out with other kids who were sneaking cigarettes or getting stoned behind the school.

They were two out-of-place misfits. It was the beginning of a great friendship.

Their high school was a lot bigger. Their schedules differed, so they made time to hang out together at lunch and on weekends.

Then came college. They both enrolled at Boston University. Rainee wanted to get her business degree in marketing. Ricky enrolled in the college of computer science. Because of their busy schedules, they arranged to hang out together at parties and rarely missed meeting in the college library on Sundays. At BU, Ricky was no longer considered a nerd and was surrounded by students with the same love. Of course, they each made other friends in college, but none as close as each other.

During their junior year, they considered renting an apartment together with two other friends. They talked about it first and made a list of pros and cons. They decided it was a good idea, since they would both save money.

Ricky won a scholarship easily because computer science was so new and there were not a lot of applicants at first. He needed some help keeping up his grades in the prerequisite courses, as he intended to get his master's degree. Rainee was of no help because all those ones and zeroes made no sense to her. One of their housemates was really good with thinking outside the box and was helpful to him. Her name was Sheila.

Rainee became a little jealous of the time Ricky was spending with her. Why? She had wondered. Why would she become jealous of Sheila? Maybe she cared a little more for Ricky than best friends and platonic buddies.

She tried to shake the feeling. Then, when a young student in one of her classes showed an interest in her, she began to understand that they would need to branch out and develop friendships beyond their little bubble. They had a long discussion and mutually agreed to expand their social lives to include others. They entered the dating scene, and even double-dated. Their relationship stayed strong throughout their four years of college.

It was not until Senior year and that fateful night of the frat party that everything changed. All it took was a few puffs on a pipe laced with PCP and awakening the next morning under the dining room table wrapped in each other's arms and half-naked.

Ricky was very attentive toward her throughout the pregnancy. By graduation night, she was showing quite a bit. However, she was not the only pregnant student graduating that year.

Joshua was born on a muggy, hot July evening at 11:30 p.m., after eight hours of labor. One week later, Ricky left for California with a computer in one hand and their baby in the other.

That was the beginning of the end of a beautiful relationship.

Six

Each of the first three days of the conference had gone well. The professor, Joshua and Zack established a routine. They met for breakfast each morning, caught the bus to the convention center, then had marvelous evenings at supper, sharing stories with other conference attendees they had met during the week.

On the morning of the last day of the conference, Joshua arose still tired from the previous night of partying, happy that the presentation was behind him.

What had kept his worry at bay was the Italian horn Professor Esposito had presented to him for good luck on the first day they arrived.

Many Italians wore the horn, called a cornicello, as a necklace pendant. The amulet was meant to insure good luck and was historically used for protection against the evil eye. This twisted horn-shaped charm was just the gesture Joshua needed to pump up his self-confidence. He was grateful for the thoughtful gift and vowed he would buy a necklace to put it on when he got the opportunity to shop. He was not a superstitious guy, but whenever he felt nervous, he would reach into his jacket pocket and rub the charm. For whatever reason, he felt it got him through his presentation.

He could now sit back and enjoy the rest of the conference. Later that afternoon he would say goodbye to Zack and Professor Esposito, and then catch a train to Venice.

Joshua noted Zack's bed was empty and supposed he had made an early start. He showered and shaved, brushed his teeth, and put on black slacks, a white long-sleeved shirt, and a tie. No need for a suit today. He was relaxed enough to dress down a little, since he would just be attending workshops and would not be in the spotlight. He made his way down to the restaurant at six-thirty to meet for breakfast with his two colleagues.

He arrived in the dining room and saw the two men standing by the entrance, apparently waiting for him.

They greeted each other, shook hands, and chose a table near the windows. Though it was early morning, the street outside the hotel was already bustling. Inside, the coffee smelled wonderful and the inviting look of pastries and croissants made Joshua's mouth water.

"Joshua, how're you feeling?" The professor asked pointing to his temple.

Joshua laughed, "Gotta tell you, other than having a little hangover, I'm feeling great now that we're done."

Professor Esposito reached across the table and patted his student's shoulder. "You were great, Joshua. Now, relax and enjoy your time."

"Yeah, you were great, bro," Zack said.

"Thanks. You're both right."

They laughed.

As color rose in his cheeks, Joshua quickly added, "I mean about relaxing and enjoying our last day together." He smiled and then ordered breakfast.

Neither of them noticed the man seated behind the professor.

He was staring at them through unusually thick sunglasses. He sipped his espresso and pretended to be reading the newspaper while he surreptitiously watched them finish their breakfast.

Bellies sated, they paid their bill and set off for the bus station.

For the last time they would catch the same bus that would take them to the conference.

The early arrival at the bus station proved to be a wise decision, as the volume of tourists was much larger than during the previous days.

Unnoticed, the man with the thick sunglasses followed them into the station to see which bus they boarded.

Joshua, Zack and the professor boarded the third bus in the line and took seats behind the driver. An almost unheard-of on-time departure of the city bus helped matters and they were soon making their way to the Palazzo Dei Congressi Conference Center. For the first few days, the ride had been just slightly over twenty minutes, but today they experienced the madness of Rome's morning rush hour.

During a frustrating forty minutes as the bus wound its way through impossibly crowded streets, Joshua began to nod off. The rhythmic rocking motion of the bus and the previous night's partying had taken its toll on him.

That was not the case for the four men who were following the bus in a blue Fiat Grande Punto.

As soon as they arrived at their stop, Joshua told Zack and Professor Esposito that he wanted to call his father. He would catch up with them in five minutes at the west entrance of the building.

The professor nodded and started walking in the direction of the conference, talking with Zack.

Joshua stepped into an alley between two large buildings and punched in the number.

"Hi, Dad. I hope I'm not calling too late. I'm on my way to the conference and I told you I'd call to tell you how my presentation went yesterday."

"Wonderful! We've been thinking about you. It's only afternoon here... 2:30ish. So how did it go?"

"Actually, really well," Josh said. "I must admit I was pretty nervous, but I felt confident about the presentation itself. I got up extra early yesterday to make sure the slides were in the right order and generally just polished up my speech."

"That's good. I knew you'd be good at it. After all, you are a naturally gifted speaker and you've been practicing this presentation for a long time." Ricky continued, "You always get nervous when you speak in public, but then you always do great.

"I know, Dad. You're right. It's just that there were so many people there— at least three hundred. Plus, you know, Professor Esposito was delivering it with me and I wanted so badly to impress him. Or at least not to embarrass him. I'm just glad it's behind me now."

Ricky laughed. "I understand. Oh, by the way, we leave for Palo Alto tomorrow. So I'll call you when we get home. The older I get, the harder these flights from Japan are."

"Yeah, I can still feel the jet-lag from the flight over to Europe."

"Did you contact Rainee again?"

"I did. It was kinda awkward at first, but you know, I think it's going to be okay. She sounded excited to meet and I am too. We'll see how it turns out. She has a room for me in a hotel in Venice, where we'll spend the weekend. It'll be cool to see Venice. I'm sure things will be good between us. Wish me luck."

"I do, Joshua. Even though I haven't kept in touch with Rainee, I have very fond memories of her. You'll get along just fine. She's a very sweet person. Besides, she helped make you. That proves that she's cool."

"Yeah, I called her after the presentation. I've gotta admit, I was pretty drunk. Zack and I were celebrating. I'm not sure I made much sense, but I got the feeling she was smiling. Truthfully, I can't remember much of that night."

"Well, you deserved to celebrate. I know how hard you worked on it. Hey, enjoy a good Chianti. Like they say: when in Rome... ."

Joshua laughed, asked his father to give his mother his love, and then said goodbye. He started walking out the alley, hoping to catch up with the professor and Zack.

He walked briskly, completely unaware of the two men closing in behind him.

A sudden blow to his head instantly rendered him unconscious.

He moaned quietly and started to come around. With his eyes still closed, he began to sense his environment. Small pebbles pressed into his back. Joshua heard angry voices in the distance. Men's voices. They were yelling at each other. Something about the time. The bad time? The wrong time? Bad timing? *Cattivo tempismo!*

The voices were coming closer and getting louder as Joshua ascended to a higher level of consciousness. He was outside. And there were smells. Stenches. Was he still in an alley? He opened his eyes a crack. A broad brick wall lay beyond his feet. The outside of a building.

Then the men were standing over him. One tall blond man about his age and one chubby, older man with a long, dark, scary-looking beard. His eyes widened. He wanted to run, but how?

"*Dammi il tuo portafoglio!*" were the first words clearly directed at him. Then the man switched to English. "Give me your wallet!"

Still, comprehension was slow in coming. For some strange reason, they were both well-dressed. One even had on a tight, Italian-styled suit. *What is happening? Why am I being robbed by these guys? They look like they don't need money.*

The tall one shoved a pistol in Joshua's face. He repeated the words in a loud voice. "I said give me your wallet!"

"Okay, okay," said Joshua. "I'll give you my wallet." He fished in his pocket, then held up his wallet. "Here."

A short, chubby man grabbed the wallet and started fishing through it to find some form of identification. He found the boy's license and handed it to the taller man.

The man nodded and the two exchanged a few more excited words in Italian.

The time it took for the men to look at his license allowed Joshua to take in his immediate environment. There were no other people around, but he did notice a blue Fiat that blocked the entrance to the alley.

There was a man behind the steering wheel. He casually watched the robbery from behind dark, thick sunglasses. Someone was watching from the back seat as well.

Joshua was not able to get a good look at either man.

The chubby man directed a subtle nod toward the car. After a moment, the other man pointed his weapon and said, "Get up!"

It did not take much persuasion, but Joshua was dizzy and slow to rise. He watched the Fiat back into the narrow alley.

One of the men quickly frisked him and took his cell phone. The tall man told him to turn around, bound Joshua's hands behind his back with a plastic zip tie.

The tall man flipped open the trunk, then pressed the gun firmly into Joshua's back. "Get in! *Velocemente!*"

Joshua was stunned, confused, and scared. "What the hell?" he said. "This isn't a robbery. Where are you taking me?" He started to yell for help.

The two men swiftly gagged his mouth with an oily-tasting rag and shoved him into the small trunk. They slammed the lid.

Darkness and exhaust fumes would become his world for the next four hours.

After being jostled about like a pinball for what seemed an eternity, the sudden smoothness of the ride indicated to Joshua that the car was now on an autostrada. His head reeled with pain. He was scared and shaken and not sure what to expect.

He knew only one thing: he had to escape.

They must know about his father's wealth. That was the only reason to kidnap him.

His eyes adjusted to the darkness. With the help of the light that managed to filter through the tail lights, he was able to make out some of the small trunk's contents. A paint can, a blanket and some rags. That was it.

Nothing of use, he thought. *Wait. If I could get my hands free, maybe I could kick out a tail light and pour the paint out of it. Other drivers might see the trail and call the police.*

It was a great idea, but nothing Joshua did loosened the zip ties. The trunk was so small that he was in a fetal position, so maneuvering his feet to kick out the tail lights became an unattainable goal. *No, this isn't the movies.* After trying everything he could, he gave up.

The car exited the autostrada and started to slow down as it made turns. Side streets and then a dirt road. Joshua was jostled around for several more minutes. Then the car slowed again and turned onto gravel. His bouncy ride came to a slow halt. The trunk was opened abruptly, allowing bright sunshine to assault his eyes.

"*Fuori! Muoviti!*" yelled one of the men. "Hurry. Out of there!"

Joshua was roughly yanked out of his small temporary prison. He stood up painfully, after being in the same cramped position for what felt like hours. He took note of his surroundings.

They were on a small street in a suburban setting. No one was around, but the men took no chances. They grabbed his arms and quickly led him into a house where others were waiting for them.

"*Congratulazioni!*" rang out from several men and one woman in the house. All shared handshakes and slaps on the back.

"Sit there!" yelled the tall Italian who was holding up his license and showing it to everyone in the room. "You see? I told you we could do it!" he boasted to the others. "Joshua Fucking Greenberg! Son of Richard Greenberg, the rich American internet– *come si dice*? tycoon– and we got him!"

Cheers and another round of congratulatory backslapping began.

Nearly thirty minutes after Joshua left them to make a call, Zack was sick with worry. He began pacing.

"Do you think something happened to him? Maybe I should go try to find him. He only went to make a call. He couldn't have gone very far. It just seems a little long for a call. Plus, it's almost nine o'clock and Joshua was very excited to hear Simon Bellows, the first speaker. He wouldn't miss him, I'm sure."

The professor nodded his head. "Yes, I'm a little worried, too, but I'm sure he's fine. Let's give him another ten minutes, all right?"

They waited the ten minutes.

"I can't wait any longer, Professor. I'm nervous."

"I understand, Zack. Let's go find him. I'm sure he's talking to his father and will be surprised to see us."

They rounded the corner of the side street and saw no one.

Zack's eyes grew wide. "He's not here! He's not here! Where could he have gone? We saw him turn in here, and he would have passed us on the way back to the building entrance. I'm going to try to call him."

Joshua's phone rang and rang. Finally Zack closed the connection as panic began to build. "No answer. What should we do?"

"Let's go inside to our seats, Zack. I'm sure we just missed him going in. Or maybe he used a different door. And don't forget, he probably turned off his cell phone in the auditorium. Either way, we'll undoubtedly find him sitting in a seat." The professor grinned. "He'll probably ask us where we've been."

Seven

Joshua would be arriving in Venice in an hour. Renee wanted to be ready. She paid her lunch tab and walked back to the hotel. Joshua was to meet her in the lobby, and she wanted to be there when he registered.

They had much to celebrate and Rainee wanted this day to be memorable. In her adjoining room was a bottle of champagne chilling in an ice bucket. Rainee ordered an assortment of hors d'oeuvres to be delivered upon his arrival: bruschetta topped with broccoli rabe pesto, pureed chickpeas, goat cheese-stuffed mushrooms with a rosemary breadcrumb topping, and crostini with roasted butternut squash, ricotta and preserves.

She wondered, *Is this too much? Am I going overboard? But there is so much to celebrate. So much to talk about.*

She sat on one of the plush settees in the lobby and watched the front door. Her thoughts turned to memories of Ricky. They had been best friends since middle school and through college. He was always there for her, always had her back. And she, his. He was funny, bright, and clever. Rainee and Ricky became known as R and R, the two most likely to stay friends forever.

Who would have thought that an act they could not even remember would change their relationship forever? But it did. Twenty-three years later, she was meeting their grown son.

Lost in her reverie of the past, Rainee just stared at the door. When she finally looked at her watch, she was surprised to see that nearly two hours had passed. Joshua was late. But no matter. She had waited this long to meet him. She could wait an hour longer.

A third hour passed and there was no sign of him. Rainee walked up to the clerk's desk. "Are there any messages for me?"

"No, signora."

Surely, he would have called if he was going to be late.

Rainee's thoughts turned into the worries of a mother. Worst-case scenarios ran through her brain. Maybe he was ill and in a hospital in Rome. Perhaps he was mugged. Could his train have derailed somewhere between Rome and Venice?

A maternal panic begin to grow. Sheattempted to quell her fears. *Get a hold of yourself. He's fine. He's still a kid. Maybe he decided to do a little sightseeing before coming to the hotel. Cool it and just call his cell phone.*

She went up to her room and retrieved his temporary number from the desk drawer.

But when she called, a computerized voice said, "This number has been disconnected."

I misdialed?

Rainee tried the number again.

"This number has been disconnected."

"What? No, that's not right," she said to no one. "I'll call Martin. Maybe Joshua called my home."

Martin detected the shakiness in Rainee's voice. "Darling, what's wrong?"

"He's not here. I tried calling but his phone is disconnected. Something's wrong. I can feel it, Martin."

"First, calm yourself. He just probably forgot to pay for more minutes. Wait a half an hour and try again. I'll do some research on the conference. I'll find out who's in charge there, and if he doesn't answer today, we'll make the call tomorrow."

"Oh my God, Martin. What if something's happened to Joshua?"

"Hold on, my love. You're anticipating the worst. Always the worrier. Let's get some facts first. I'll do my research, then start making calls tomorrow morning, since it's likely too late to speak with anyone tonight. Try not to fear the worst. Get some sleep."

"Like that's going to happen." She instantly regretted her sarcastic tone.

"Yes, I know you, but this is not a bloody mystery novel, Rainee. It's probably some sort of technical glitch. Rain, have you eaten any supper?"

"Not yet. I couldn't now. I've lost my appetite."

"Eat something, even if it's only bread. Doctor's orders."

"Okay. Martin, call me as early as possible. I'll call you if he shows up."

"It'll be okay, Rainee. I love you."

She thanked him for attempting to calm her down and told him she loved him too.

Rainee called down to the front desk and asked the clerk to notify her when Joshua showed up, no matter what time it was. He assured her he would call her.

She began to pace the room.

After all he is just a twenty-three year old alone in a country he's never been in, a place where he doesn't speak the language. Of course, he's probably well-traveled. They have the money to take trips anywhere in the world. Ricky would have wanted his child to be well-rounded, and would have introduced him to diverse cultures. But anything might have happened, and it's possible he doesn't know what to do!

Long ago, Rainee learned to trust her instincts. Those instincts helped her get through many events in her life. When she became a mother to little Jana, they seemed to heighten even more. Those maternal feelings intensified now as an intuition of dread overcame her.

Something was wrong, and she knew it.

Eight

Rainee wondered how hard could it be to locate a phone number for one Richard Greenberg? He lived in Palo Alto, California. He semi-retired very comfortably when a major internet company bought his business and retained him as a consultant. He was a well-known philanthropist. His name was on the Board of Directors for several non-profit organizations. He was all over the web. But his number was unlisted.

Rainee decided to call the police in his city.

"Palo Alto Police Department. Please hold." It was a woman's voice.

"But—" Rainee was annoyed. "Damn it!" She waited impatiently while a series of beeps reminded her that she was on hold.

"Palo Alto Police Department. May I help you?" The receptionist's deep raspy voice reminded Rainee of someone who probably had smoked cigarettes all her life.

"Yes, I want to report a missing person. I am calling from Italy. Please do not put me on hold again."

"Please hold."

Rainee was about to scream into the phone, when she heard a series of clicks, and then a man's deep voice, "Sergeant Lawrence speaking."

"Thank you. I need to get in touch with a Mr. Richard Greenberg of your city. But he's unlisted. It's imperative that I speak with him. I believe his son is missing."

"Your name, please."

"My name is Rainee Allen. Mr. Greenberg is... uh... an old friend of mine. I'm calling from Venice, Italy."

"If you're a friend, you should have his number."

"Sergeant, we haven't spoken for many years. Our son... his son, Joshua, is in Italy. He came over for a conference. We were to meet in Venice. That was yesterday. He hasn't shown up and I'm really worried."

"Uh huh." Rainee could hear paper being shifted around. "Your name again, ma'am?"

"Rainee Allen."

"Spell it."

Exasperated, she spelled it out for him.

She could hear him scribbling on paper. "Rainee Allen, the writer?"

"Yes." She sighed.

"Yeah, I read your first book. Good mystery."

"Sergeant Lawrence, let me give you my number here. Call Mr. Greenberg. He will verify that Joshua is supposed to be meeting me. Please!"

"Okay, okay. Calm down. Give me your number. I will call you back. And ma'am, this had better be legit."

Rainee paced in her room, not knowing what to do next. She knew Ricky had all the assets at his disposal to find Joshua. Money would not be an object.

Deep in thought, she was startled by the ringing phone. "Yes, ma'am. This is Sergeant Lawrence. Xavier Lawrence of the Palo Alto Police Department. Sorry, but the housekeeper said Mr. and Mrs. Greenberg have been in Asia. They are in route, probably somewhere over the Pacific. Won't be back until late tonight."

"Oh no!"

"She did, however, corroborate your story about their son."

"Sergeant, what should I do? I know very little about Joshua." She started pacing again.

"I would advise you to go to the Italian police with it. Tell them your story. I can send a picture. His picture was in our local paper for working with some professor. Meanwhile, I will advise Mr. Greenberg of the situation when he lands. He's kind of a big name around these parts. Big donor to the Police Foundation. In fact, I will personally meet him at the airport."

"Thank you, Sergeant."

Nine

Rainee took the first flight out to Rome the next morning. She walked the mosaic-tiled floor to the noir glass door marked *Dipartimento Investigativo*. As she opened it, the odors of leather, sweat, and espresso swirled around her.

The officer who took Rainee's complaint told her she had just missed a few cooler April days, followed by this unusual heat wave. He apologized that there was no air-conditioning. The police station, like many old buildings in Italy, dated back to before electricity.

All the iron-barred, frosted windows were opened wide to allow some circulation, but the air remained hot and stagnant. Beads of sweat formed on her neck and brow.

Detective Fabrizio Piscitelli spoke English well, and he showed sympathy and patience with the American. His dark hair and olive-complected skin illuminated his white teeth. His chin was strong, and his brown eyes were focused on her face. There was some graying at his temples, the beginning of a receding hairline, and just a few frown lines.

Rainee was astonished at how quickly things were moving. There was already a printed flyer with Joshua's face on it. She guessed they had mobilized thanks to a call from Sergeant Lawrence back at the PAPD and because Joshua was the son of a well-known figure.

Detective Piscitelli addressed his handpicked team in a packed squad room. Many of the officers wiped the sweat from their brows and some even used the printed flyer to fan themselves. Piscitelli showed no sign that the heat bothered him. While sweat stains formed on other officer's uniforms, he did not even loosen his tie or take off his jacket. He projected confidence and control. That was what Rainee needed— someone who could take control, as she was losing hers.

After briefing them, he added, "We have not yet received any calls regarding a ransom. Pursue any lead you get, no matter how small."

When he dismissed the group, Piscitelli sat down again with Rainee. "Tell me about your history with this boy," he asked.

"Why? How is that relevant?"

"I assure you, it is relevant, Ms. Allen. Every detail we can gather is important."

"I... I really don't know Joshua, but... I was hoping to get to know him."

Piscitelli raised his eyebrows.

"No, no, it's not like that at all. He is my son. I gave him up for adoption twenty-three years ago. He contacted me and wanted to get to know me. Me, his biological mother. I wanted the same, so I agreed to meet him in Venice."

"I see. Why do you look familiar? Is your face on one of our wanted posters?" He raised his eyebrows and laughed at his own joke.

Rainee did not find it funny. She sighed. "As you already know, my name is Rainee Allen. I'm a writer."

Piscitelli sat up, "Ah, si, the Nazi trial?"

Distressed by chit-chat, she nodded. "Look, Detective, shouldn't you be out there looking for Joshua? Talking with people from the conference? What about Professor Esposito or his friend, Zack? Um, Abare... no, no... Abee. Yes, Zachary Abee. They were the last people to see him. I'm sure they could answer your questions better than—"

"They have been detained and have already been interviewed."

"Detained? Are they here?" She looked around the room. "Where are they? I want to speak with them."

"They were driven to the scene of the alleged crime. Our detectives will... *come si dice?...* brush the area."

"Comb?"

"*Scusami?*"

"You mean comb the area. Surely they are not under suspicion, are they?"

"We rule nothing out. But it's unlikely. Protocol, Ms. Allen, we must follow it. For instance, according to his friend, the night before he disappeared, they got very drunk."

"Yes, he called me. He was celebrating. His presentation was earlier that day."

"Si, I know. Zachary might recall a conversation they had that strangers might have overheard. Any part of that conversation could help in the investigation. Unfortunately, Zachary was also drunk and cannot remember much of what occurred that evening.

What we do know is that Joshua returned to the hotel. He received a wake-up call and left the hotel to have breakfast. He rode a bus to the convention hall with Zack and Professor Esposito, then excused himself to make a phone call. He was not seen after that. It is all in the details. We try not to overlook anything."

Ten

Morning followed a night of interrupted sleep.

Joshua hadn't stopped shaking since he was left alone in a dark room several hours before. His thoughts roamed from his father to Deborah to Rainee in an endless loop throughout the interminably long night. Not knowing what would happen next kept him at a level of fear he had never known. He was scared, and worse, alone. He even found himself praying to God for help.

All was quiet throughout the house. It was a stark contrast to the night of raucous partying he had listened to from the tiny, dark, and locked room that would be his home for the next few days.

Joshua lay on his side on a hard bed with his hands and feet tied. He peered into the darkness to try to familiarize himself with the little room.

It was simply too dark, with little ambient light. He could see nothing but three cinderblock walls and a small bed when the men carried him into what he thought was a pantry. He had not been focusing on anything at that moment but his own fear.

At some point late into the night, he had managed to lower his body to the floor and squirm around to try to picture his environment, hoping his eyes had adjusted well enough to the darkness. The room was very small. The twin-sized bed barely fit and there was no other furniture. The floor was cold and dirty. He sat back on the edge of the bed and started to cry. The crying continued until he fell into an exhausted sleep.

The night was endlessly long. Joshua awoke many times, each accompanied by a sick feeling in the pit of his stomach when he realized his nightmare was not a dream. *How in the world did this happen?*

His thoughts continuously returned to his father who, he knew, would be so deeply distressed and heartbroken.

He had a wonderful relationship with his father that had blossomed as he grew into a young man. It had not always been that way.

Like so many boys, Joshua was impetuous and as some of his public school friends often noted, spoiled. When he entered junior high school, he began to realize that he was different than some of his classmates. He was dropped off by either his mother or father in expensive cars, he always had the latest in clothes, and electronic games. The family vacationed each year in Europe, Asia, or on islands throughout the world that are known for their beauty and expensive hotels. It was the only life he knew.

Thankfully, his dad was a very patient, loving and understanding parent who knew that his son would eventually grow into the grounded man he had become. He was right.

With that last thought, he drifted off to sleep once again.

Eleven

Detective Piscitelli convinced Rainee to go back to her hotel. "Signora Allen, if he was kidnapped, we will hear from his captors for a ransom. They may contact you."

"How? His phone is disconnected."

"Si, but he would have saved your number in the phone. They can power it on and find that number. Let us hope that is what they do."

Hesitantly, she acquiesced.

The first thing Rainee did when she returned to her room was to plug in her phone. She wanted to keep it charged, so she could answer it at any time. She checked for messages, but there were none.

She lay down on her bed, but knew she would not nap. How could she? Her brain was still abuzz with many different scenarios of what might have happened to Joshua.

The Grand Hotel de la Minerve was situated in a very busy section of Rome. Martin had done his research and located the hotel in which Joshua and Zack had stayed. Wanting something a bit nicer for his wife, he booked her into this five-star hotel, only a block away.

It had once been a mansion and was dated back to the 1600s. The suite had a very large bedroom, a living room and one and a half marble bathrooms. Rainee admired the coffered ceiling which had been hand-painted. The suite combined a contemporary style while still keeping with old charm. There was even a private terrace.

When she stepped outside to inspect her view, the bustling, noisy city, made her turn around and close the doors. Rome was not one of Rainee's favorite places. Street sounds pervaded her thoughts. Honking horns, sirens, loud vendors were all sounds she tried to block unsuccessfully. Rainee was not there as a tourist. She was now on a mission. She began pacing the room.

When Rainee wrote her novels, she edited aloud her written words. Her thoughts became better organized in her head. She tried the same as she methodically pieced together what had transpired.

She paced the room. "Okay, what are the facts? According to Professor Esposito, they always boarded the same bus to the conference together. He arrived at the conference, then went to make a call. But to whom? Probably to call Ricky. He wasn't seen after his call.

What the hell happened to him? We know the police checked the hospitals with no success. That's good. I think that's good. But people don't just disappear. If he was kidnapped, why has no one called about a ransom?"

By timely chance, the phone rang. Rainee jumped at the sound. Instinctively, she picked up the hotel telephone. There was just a dial tone, yet the ringing continued. She realized it was her cell phone.

She quickly grabbed the flip phone. "Hello? Joshua?"

It was a man with a deep voice. "No. Who is this?"

"My name is Rainee Allen. Who are you?"

"I have called because we have Joshua Greenberg."

"What do you mean you have him? Can I talk with him? Please?"

The man hesitated. He muffled the mouthpiece for a moment. Then he said, "No. We have him and I am calling to demand money for his return."

"Please, I need to speak with him. How do I know you have him? How do I know he's still alive?"

There was more silence. The phone had been muffled, but Rainee could hear someone arguing. Finally, Joshua's voice came on the phone. "Rainee?"

"Oh my God! Joshua, are you okay?" The man with the deep voice said, "Enough talk. You have your proof. We will contact you again with our demands. Lunga vita Brigate Rosse!"

The phone went silent.

Twelve

Ricky and Deborah were exhausted when they stepped off the plane. It had been a long flight home. Happily, all their suitcases arrived. Ricky collected them, then they went through Customs.

They stepped outside and breathed the refreshing San Francisco air. Expecting their driver, Ricky was surprised when Sergeant Lawrence approached. "Mr. Greenberg?"

The grim look on the police officer's face scared him.

"Officer! What—"

"Mr. and Mrs. Greenberg, I need to speak with you. It's about your son."

"Joshua? Is he okay? I spoke with him yesterday. I think it was yesterday." Ricky looked at his wife. "Deborah, was it yesterday?"

As Sergeant Lawrence related the facts, Ricky felt his knees start to buckle.

"Sit down, Honey," Deborah said and guided him to a nearby bench.

Despair flashed across Ricky's face. He looked up at Sergeant Lawrence. "What can we do? What happens next?"

"Ms. Allen is working closely with the Rome police department. I emailed them Joshua's picture. Now that you're back, I would advise you to get in touch with her." He offered a slip of paper. "Here, I've written down her number."

Ricky frowned. "I've got to get to Rome right away. We're here at the airport. I'll go book my ticket."

"Ricky, darling, let's go home and get your medicine first. Maybe take a nap. You're exhausted. It won't take that long, and I can pack you a fresh set of clothes."

He nodded. "Of course. I'll book a private jet. Call Anne, my assistant. Have her do that. I can be back here in just a few hours." He turned to the officer. "Thanks, Sergeant."

"No problem, Mr. Greenberg. Can I give you a lift home?"

"Thanks, but I have a car picking us up." He glanced past the officer as a blue Lexus stopped at the curb. "Oh, here it is now."

"Anything the department can do to help, call me directly. My personal number is on that paper."

"Thanks, Sergeant."

Ricky was gaining control of his emotions. His mind went into problem-solving mode, methodically planning each necessary step to find Joshua. The ride back to Palo Alto was very quiet, except for Deborah's sobbing.

Ricky put his arm around Deborah. "I'll find him. I promise. Whatever it takes. I'll bring Josh home."

Ricky took out his cell phone and pressed the power button. He was not surprised to see forty-five messages waiting for him.

He scrolled down to a European phone number and compared it to the number Officer Lawrence gave him.

Sure enough, it was Rainee's.

Thirteen

The door opened. Silhouetted in the light was a young, thin, tall, dark-haired woman. She gestured harshly. "Get up! Get up, rich boy! *Piangere non serve a niente!* Stop crying! Are you a baby?" she said as she entered the room.

Joshua looked up.

"You, little baby, are going to make us rich! Daddy will pay big money for his spoiled little boy."

Joshua flinched as she sat down at the foot of the bed.

She snickered. "Do not worry. I will not bite you. Did you sleep?"

These were the first thoughtful words he had heard since he was taken. "On and off," he answered.

"You hungry? I will get you breakfast."

Wow, I am starving, thought Joshua. *I haven't eaten since yesterday's breakfast.*

"Yes, please. I'm really hungry, but I need to pee even more."

The woman looked at him quizzically and asked what he meant.

"I need to urinate. Is there a toilet I can use?"

"Oh. Si, I will take you to one." She knelt, untied Joshua's feet, then cut the zip tie that bound his hands. "Do not try anything stupid. There are a lot of people in this house who would not like that."

"I won't," he said.

He stood up and started with the woman toward the door, but before they reached it, a tall man burst in. Joshua recognized him as one of his abductors.

"What the... *Che cazzo stai facendo?*" He yelled at the woman. "Are you crazy? Why did you untie him? What the fuck are you doing, you stupid woman?"

He slapped her hard across the face with the back of his hand and she went flying backward onto the bed. Her left cheek began to redden.

Joshua stood there stunned.

Holding her cheek, the woman yelled, "He needs the Water Closet, you asshole!"

The man stepped forward to hit her again, but stopped short and brought his arm down slowly, struggling to control himself. Positioned menacingly over her, he pointed a finger close to her face. "Do not ever untie him unless I say to do it. Do you understand?"

She looked up at him with hate in her eyes. She slapped his hand away and slowly stood, holding her cheek. "I am going to get ice."

The man grabbed Joshua's arm, pulled him out of the room, and took him to the WC. Joshua was shaken, but grateful to be able to relieve himself. He was returned, without breakfast, to the room by the same man, who then re-tied his hands and feet.

He was alone again.

Fourteen

Detective Piscitelli was pacing in Rainee's hotel room. "Brigate Rosse. That is the Red Brigade. They broke up years ago, but there are smaller factions associated with them."

"What do I tell them when they call? Joshua sounded so scared. God, I hope they don't hurt him."

"Just keep them on the line as long as you can. Let me take down the number they called from. Maybe we can trace it. It's our only lead so far." He gestured toward the other officer in the room. "This officer is Detective Adamoli."

Rainee nodded to the other man.

His black curly hair matched his curly mustache. He hooked up wires to Rainee's cell phone, then set up his computer and other equipment.

Detective Piscitelli said, "He will stay with you and trace any incoming calls. Please do not leave this room."

"Okay but I didn't bring my laptop. Could I borrow one? I want to research the Brigate Rosse. I'll go crazy with nothing to do but wait for a call."

"Si, use this one." He handed her one of the many pieces of electronic equipment which had been brought to the hotel.

When Piscitelli left, Rainee called Martin on the room phone and reported everything. She asked him to only call her hotel phone line, wanting to keep the cell line open at all times.

Martin asked, "Do you want me to come to Rome, my love? I can have my receptionist cancel my patients."

"No. I love you for offering, but there's nothing you can do here that isn't already being done. I'll be fine. But please give little Jana kisses and hugs from her mommy."

Detective Adamoli was a quiet man who knew very little English. When Rainee talked, he smiled a lot and nodded, but she carried on the solo conversation anyway.

Waiting was unnerving for Rainee. She resigned herself to researching the Brigate Rosse. If she had been nervous before, the information she found online caused her even more worry. She exclaimed to Adamoli, "Oh my God, these people are so dangerous! They're extremists."

He only nodded and smiled.

When her cell phone finally rang, Rainee jumped.

The detective was ready. He pushed a button and nodded his permission to proceed.

She picked up the phone. "This is Rainee Allen."

"Ciao, Signora Allen. We have our demands and instructions."

Rainee grabbed a pen. "I'm ready."

"We are demanding five million Euros in unmarked cash. We know who his father is, so we know we can get that. You have two days to come up with the money."

Rainee could not come up with that kind of money. She felt panicked and unsure of what to say next.

The man on the phone said, "Signora, did you hear what I said?"

"I did, yes. I did, but I need more time than that. I cannot reach his father. He's on a business trip in Japan. And it is Friday. Even if I could find him, the banks will close. You must give us more time. Please. I beg you."

The phone was muffled again. The voice said calmly, "Si. We will give you four days. That is all."

"Thank you. Oh, thank you so much. Grazie. Where do you want the cash brought?"

"*Firenze*. We will talk again in two days with new instructions."

"Firenze. That's Florence, right?'

"Si."

"All right. Please, please, per favore, may I speak with Joshua again? I need to hear his voice."

"No! In four days, you can speak to him. In four days."

"Grazie, and—" The sudden click surprised Rainee. She looked at the detective.

He was on his phone calling his sergeant. He was speaking quickly, which only added to Rainee's fears.

"Did you get it? Do you have a location?"

In fractured English, he said, "Si, but is not Roma. In Firenze. I go now to the station."

"I'm coming with you."

Adamoli sped to the station. The sound of the squad car's siren echoed through the air, and one hand blasted the horn. Otherwise they rode in silence.

Rainee's mind swirled with thoughts. Above all was her concern for Joshua's safety. But she reasoned that since they promised he could speak in four days, he must be okay. Then there was the issue of the money. Five million Euros was well over five million American dollars. But Ricky would produce the money necessary to get his son back.

Rainee would buy another phone to keep the line open and still stay in touch with Martin and Ricky.

She took out her pad and wrote down a list of what needed to be done. Not an easy task riding over the potholes and crumbling asphalt of the Eternal City. Her pen kept jumping off the paper.

The station was hopping, crowded, and still uncomfortably hot. Adamoli directed her to an empty desk, where she observed the action happening around her.

More investigators had been called in. They were agents from Interpol who wore suits and ties that reminded Rainee of the FBI. They stood out among the Italian police, whose sleeves were rolled up and unbuttoned shirts were sweat-stained. If it was a different occasion, Rainee would find it comical. Her fingers uncontrollably tapped the desktop with nervous energy.

The Interpol officers explained to her that the phone signal indicated Florence, but not an exact location. The kidnappers' base of operations could be in one of the many villages that surrounded the city. The operation would move to Florence and hope that with the next call, they would get a stronger signal pinpointing their location.

Piscitelli and the lead agent argued.

Rainee assumed it was because Florence was out of Piscitelli's jurisdiction. Then he left the room in a hurry with an annoyed but determined look on his face.

Rainee pulled back her shoulders and addressed the agent who had been arguing with Piscitelli. "Excuse me, sir. Are you aware that Joshua is my biological son?"

The room became quiet as heads turned to look at Rainee.

He shook her hand, introduced himself, and handed her his business card. "Agent Roger Harrington from Interpol. London office. You must be—" He looked down at his report, "—Rainee Allen. Good to meet you. We are just now getting all the logistics of this case. Apologies. We did not know that Richard Greenberg is your husband."

"Richard Greenberg is not my husband, but he was my friend."

"In light of this additional information, I think we have more to discuss. Please, have a seat." He pulled out a chair for her, and then called to a detective to get some blood drawn. "We will need your DNA. It may help us when we get close to Joshua."

"Why? Oh..." Rainee shuddered when she realized that DNA was used to identify bodies.

The men in the room slowly got busy with their work and noise began to fill the air once again.

Her cell phone rang, and everyone stopped and turned to Rainee again.

Adamoli nodded at her, and she pressed the talk button. "This is Rainee Allen."

The solemn voice at the other end said, "Rainee, it's Ricky."

His familiar voice caused a sense of relief to run through her body. "Ricky! Thank God." An overpowering flood of tears poured out. "Oh, Ricky."

"I'm coming, Rainee. I'll be there soon."

Fifteen

Nap? How could he nap? Ricky was too wound up to get some much-needed sleep. Not knowing how long he would be gone, he gathered enough medicines to last a month. His assistant, Shannon, had reserved a private jet and told him it would be fueled and ready to take off within the hour. Rainee had asked him to meet her in Florence.

He hugged his wife goodbye and promised again he would bring Joshua home. He threw his bag into his 1967 Jaguar coupe and backed out of his driveway.

Ricky drove through town running yellow lights and barely stopping for stop signs. He showed little regard for the rules of the road. Not once did he look into his mirror to see if he may have left any accidents in his wake.

His wheels squealed as he took a right turn onto the frontage road which led to the highway.

There were no cars on the on-ramp, so Ricky downshifted and sped up. His mind was on Joshua and not on the road. By the time he checked his side-view mirror as he approached the entrance of the highway, it was too late to avoid the semi-trailer truck barreling up on his left side.

The Jaguar sideswiped the oversized truck. Ricky found himself flying upside-down. The car landed hard on its side and slid into a ditch. Blackness descended.

Sergeant Lawrence heard about the crash on the police radio and hurried to the Greenberg's home to inform Deborah. She was stunned and felt faint, but he caught her and led her to a chair. "Don't worry, Mrs. Greenberg. He's in good hands. They'll take good care of him. I can drive you to the hospital. Then I'll contact Ms. Allen and let her know what's happened."

When he came to, Ricky had been admitted to Palo Alto Hospital. As the attendants wheeled him down the hall into surgery, Deborah walked by his side. She whispered, "Everything is going to be all right, Ricky."

His mouth was dry, his body in pain, and he could taste blood on his lips. "Where... where am I?"

"Don't talk, darling. Save your energy. You were in an accident. You crashed into a semi when you were merging onto the highway. You're in the hospital. They're taking you into surgery. Oh, my darling..." Deborah began to cry.

He begged, "No, no. I have to go to Joshua. I have to find him. Don't let them put me out." He was struggling to stay awake, but the anesthetic dripping into his veins overcame him. He passed out as his gurney reached the operating room.

Sixteen

The news of Ricky's accident hit Rainee like a punch in the gut. She was concerned for Ricky, but more concerned for Joshua. Without Ricky, how would she get the money for the ransom?

In shock, Rainee relayed the information to the detectives.

Swears in Italian and a lot of hand waving filled the air. *Cazzo! Dannazione!*

Detective Piscitelli had returned to the room, very much back in charge. He took Rainee's arm and led her to a chair. "Can I get you anything, Signora Allen?"

She forced a smile. "Grazie. Just help me understand what we can do. Do we tell the kidnappers? Do we keep it from them? What's next?"

"I am not sure. First, we have to get everyone— *come si dice?*— up to tempo?"

"Speed."

"*Scusami?*"

"You meant to say up to speed, not tempo." Rainee regretted her correction immediately. "I'm so sorry. Force of habit. Occupational hazard."

"I promise you we will come up with a plan. Come with me. I will call a meeting. We must do this before you get your next call."

All the detectives gathered for the newest briefing armed with lots of espresso and cigarettes.

Rainee noted that the agents from Interpol were not present.

Voices gradually rose as strategizing and arguing filled the smoky room.

It appeared to Rainee that no one agreed on anything. Her concern for Joshua was raising her blood pressure and she thought she was going to explode.

"Hey!"

No one heard her.

"Hey!" she said louder.

Still no one acknowledged her. She grabbed a police whistle that was on a nearby desk and blew into it. The shrill sound stopped everyone instantly. All eyes turned toward her.

"You are not going to get anything accomplished if you don't work together. Now please sit down. I have something to say."

Some of the men took a seat, surprised by her commanding presence.

She was shaking with distress. After all, who was she to talk this way to the police? All she knew was that Joshua was in trouble and no amount of shouting would accomplish anything.

"I know you have protocols for this type of event, but it's obvious that you are not talking to each other. You are talking around each other. Over each other. No one is listening to the other. I will be getting a phone call any time now and I want a definitive plan of action. I need to know what to say to these people. I need to know now!"

Silence filled the room. The men were a little stunned by a woman taking control of the situation.

Detective Piscitelli was the first to speak up. "Si, Signora Allen is correct." With a nod to Rainee, he continued. "We must cooperate and come up with a plan immediately."

Everyone nodded.

"Let us separate into three groups, then meet in thirty minutes, listen to each plan, and settle on just one course of action. In total agreement." There was some grumbling, but fifteen men left the room, determined to return with a plan.

Before he left the room, Piscitelli said, "Signora, you have a good head on your shoulders. I know how fearful you are for your son. How are you holding it together?"

"Detective, I have no idea."

Thirty minutes passed quickly, and the men ambled back into the room, still talking.

Each group related their plan of action.

Piscitelli interpreted for Rainee.

There was some disagreement about two of the plans, and only one stood out as being the most promising.

They all doubted that the kidnappers would know Ricky's plight. It had not made the Italian papers. At least not yet. That was considered by all to be a good thing.

When the phone call came, Rainee was to agree to everything the kidnappers demanded. Though the Italian police knew she could not come up with the five million Euros, Rainee would agree anyway. She would have to explain that she was in touch with Joshua's father and that he would fly the money out personally. However, for him to liquidate his assets into cash would take an additional couple of days. She would also warn them that if they hurt Joshua in any way, the deal was off, and she would bring in the authorities.

They all agreed the plan was plausible. The kidnappers had already agreed to extra days. The plan could only work if they allowed a few more days, and if word of Richard Greenberg's accident did not make the news. With social media becoming accessible to everyone nowadays, there was no predicting what they would or would not know.

The operation moved to Florence. Detective Piscitelli worked in collaboration with the Florence police, and a hotel suite was ready and waiting for Rainee when they pulled into the city.

The hotel was not nearly as opulent as the previous ones. However, the room was a suite and had space. Lots of it. Rainee noted that furniture must have been removed to create the extra space. Folding tables and chairs were set up, telephone lines were strewn across the floor and an ashtray was placed on every available surface. She even noticed bags of food lying on the floor in one corner of the room.

It was a practical hotel choice, one that was usually used for business conferences. So the police posted a sign in the lobby—*Consiglio Nazionale Ingegneri*— which translated to National Council of Engineers. Still a male-dominated field, it would cover the comings and goings of the officers in plain clothes.

Computers and wires were hooked up to tap Rainee's cell phone. The smell of coffee and cigarettes co-mingled so strongly that Rainee kept the windows wide open. She was told not to leave for fear she would be recognized and followed by one of the kidnappers.

Rainee did not have to be told that. She had no intention of moving away from her phone.

Nighttime brought recurring nightmares of harm coming to Joshua, so she gave up on sleep. She kept in touch with Sergeant Lawrence for updates on Ricky.

He reported that they had to use the jaws-of-life to get him out of his mangled vehicle. His left leg was badly injured, but the surgery was successful. If Ricky wanted to be able to walk again, he would need to keep his leg immobilized for at least six weeks.

There were metal pins sticking out of his leg. The doctors called it external fixation, which was used to stabilize bone and soft tissues. He was kept highly medicated. Sergeant Lawrence said it was a miracle that he was even alive. He added that Deborah was a wreck and would not leave her husband's side.

Rainee was discouraged by the news, and after she searched the computer for images of external fixation, she was even more worried.

Martin called every day, and Rainee kept him abreast of the news. She assured him that she was being taken care of by the Italian police and wanted him to remain with little Jana, who was missing her mother.

Martin knew the stress his wife was under and wanted to prescribe some anti-anxiety medicine, but she refused his offer. "Honey, I can get through this without meds. They will only screw up my mind, and I have to be able to think clearly."

Thinking clearly with little to no sleep was a near impossibility, but Martin understood Rainee's determination. "Whatever you need, my love. You know I'm here for you."

She knew and was grateful.

Seventeen

It was two hours or more before Joshua saw or heard anyone. The silence was broken by noise from a group of people he thought might be in a room right above his. They seemed to be arguing as the volume of their discussion increased steadily. Something was going on, and he didn't understand Italian.

He waited quietly for a while, but then his world was turned upside down as three men flung the door open. They ran into his room accompanied by the woman from before.

"Get up! We are moving!"

Joshua did as he was told.

"Donald Duck, untie his feet," commanded the same man who had taken him to the bathroom. Then he turned to the woman. "Daisy, get his things," he barked.

He appeared to Joshua to be the leader of the group. Not only did it seem like he was the most aggressive of them, he was also well over six feet tall and very powerfully built. And at this moment, he was clearly angry. Everyone jumped to his command.

Donald Duck? Daisy? mused Joshua. It became obvious to him that they were using these names to protect their identities. It seemed especially strange— almost comical— to Joshua that they would use cartoon names, but he figured that everyone knew these American cartoon characters. And after all, they had kidnapped an American.

He was thrown roughly into a faded yellow van with darkened windows on one side. Joshua was made to lie on the floor between the front and second rows of seats. Three men and the woman he had met earlier were also in the van. They backed out of a driveway, and then were off to the next destination.

The group spoke to each other sparingly— and always in Italian— so he could not understand much of what they said, but he did hear one familiar word: *mangia*. That brought back his hunger in an almost painful way. Since he had not had anything to eat in over thirty hours, he felt faint and weak. Now there was a possibility of fixing that. The car bumped over railroad tracks, jostling him. They drove in relative silence before they came to a stop.

Two of the men and the woman got out of the van.

The woman asked Joshua if he wanted some chicken and a drink.

He looked at her and nodded.

She nodded back and slid the van door shut. Several minutes passed in silence before they returned.

Daisy asked the leader called Mickey Mouse if she could untie Joshua's hands so he could eat. "No!" he responded. "You feed him!"

She glared at the leader and started to remove the food from the bags.

There was very little conversation for most of the drive. Joshua chewed the food that Daisy fed him slowly, savoring each bite. His wrists were bleeding from the ties and he was very uncomfortable in his position on the floor, but he said nothing.

A conversation started between the men in the front seats. He understood very little, but every now and again, he would recognize some words. The word *castello* came up several times. He felt sure it meant castle but couldn't figure out why they were using it. He also thought he heard a reference to *Romeo e Giulietta*, but that confused him even more.

The journey to their next stop took about a half-hour. Joshua could tell they drove through a populated area— a city, he supposed by the sound of horns honking and the smell of fuel. He lifted his head to try to see out the front window. Someone slapped the back of his head and he lowered his eyes and nose to the floor, inhaling a blend of stale cigarettes and dirt.

Shortly it became rural and they were driving along a country road. The van came to a sudden stop, and the leader got out of the vehicle and yelled at someone. It sounded to Joshua that a heard of cows were being led from their pasture. Mickey Mouse got back into the van, swearing, and slammed the door in anger. The driver cracked open a window to admit a breeze. Joshua detected the odor of cow manure and grass. The van jerked forward and soon after they pulled onto a bumpy gravel driveway and stopped.

Everyone but Joshua exited the vehicle. He could hear several voices as he lay in a fetal position on the floor of the van.

Welcoming chatter filled the air. "*Benvenuti, amici! E' fantastico rivedervi. Come e' andato il viaggio? Ci sono posti di blocco ovunque. E' per questo che avete fatto tardi?*"

From the sounds, Joshua guessed there were five or six men and one woman in total. He saw that he was right when they dragged him out of the vehicle and onto a front porch.

It was an old white wooden farmhouse with weathered wood beams and large dead plants on either side of a big metal-framed screen door. A broken-down tractor and two dismantled and rusted old cars littered the grounds. There was a cow munching on grass, but little else that he could see. Farther in the distance was the shell of what may have once been another farm house.

Mickey Mouse roughly grabbed Joshua. "Here he is. Our ticket to freedom. Our banker!"

The others laughed and slapped the backs of the visiting men.

A balding man with a stained and wrinkled apron came out of the house drying his hands. He looked quite a bit older than those Joshua had traveled with. Fortunately, he spoke passable English and he was civil, even nice. The man took drink orders from the others and offered Joshua a beer.

Joshua refused, surprised that the man was pleasant to him. He asked for a glass of water instead.

Everyone went inside. Joshua was led to a small wooden chair in the living room. They cut his zip ties. He listened to them talk and laugh with each other. His fear lessened, and he became observant of his surroundings. He tried to notice every detail, just in case it might be useful later. Unfortunately, the old farmhouse was simple and nondescript. The walls were rough, with peeled mint-green paint and the furniture old and tattered. An unplugged portable television was sitting on a wooden crate in one corner. He noticed long colorful beads— the kind often seen in the sixties— hanging in one of the doorways. They were the only object in the room contributing any color at all. Stale cigarette smell emanated from the faded carpet, and scrunched paper cups were strewn around a filled waste basket. A reshaped wire hanger hung over the basket and pierced the wall. There was no chance of anyone here being recruited by the NBA.

The sound of a car approaching on gravel caused everyone to stop talking.

One man looked through a hole in the curtains to see who was approaching. He nodded back at the group and stepped outside.

Mickey Mouse motioned to Daisy to take Joshua down to the room that had been prepared for him. She nodded, stood up and tugged Joshua on the arm. "Get up! *Andiamo, cerca di muoverti*!"

She led him downstairs through a stone-walled basement the width of the house. She fiddled with keys and unlocked a cold, dank-smelling, and windowless room that likely had been a root cellar.

Mold grew on one of the exterior walls. Any hole in the ground tended to fill with water. Joshua said, "Great. I get to inhale mold. How many floods has this basement seen?"

The room itself was practically empty, but it did have a mattress on the floor, two bottles of water, and an empty pail. At least it was a real bed, albeit with no springs, and real pillows. He'd had so little sleep since he was taken, he was looking forward to sleeping on the mattress once the woman left him alone. He hoped she would simply close the door and leave.

He got his wish.

The screen door squeaked open and everyone in the room stood out of respect. A white-haired man entered, scanned the room, and nodded to each person there. The older contingent went to greet him with handshakes and back-slapping. He motioned for everyone to sit as he took a seat.

He held his voice to a whisper and spoke only in Italian. "Address me only as Signore E."

Everyone pulled their chairs closer to hear him.

Signore E. asked the leader, "Well, what is your plan now that the police figured out that you were in Florence, eh?" He shook his index finger at Mickey Mouse. "I knew it was a stupid idea to arrange the drop where you live! You must start listening to me, Tomasso! When I ran this organization back in the '80s, we were smarter than you young punks!" He shook his head in disapproval. "You are a child! You need to start behaving like an adult— a smart adult— if you expect this plan of yours to work! Listen to me from now on or you are doomed to fail!"

Tomasso sat quietly, his head down as the older man chastised him.

I fucking hate him! thought the younger man. *He had a couple of successes back in the dark ages, so he thinks he knows the answers to everything? Well, fuck him! He does not!*

Tomasso's anger grew as he listened to the man drone on. When he had enough, he stood up, threw up his hands and said, "Okay, okay, Uncle! I get it. You know everything! You are the boss! I am just a fucking idiot, right?"

"That is not what I said."

"Well, I got the kid, no? I took him in the middle of a busy city, in the middle of the day, and I am going to get us a lot of money because I did this!"

"Our plan was a good one."

"This is my plan. Not yours! Stop badgering me, old man." Tomasso turned and started to leave the room to join others in the kitchen.

The old man said, "I was successful! I kidnapped Aldo Moro! And the American general! My plans worked because I was careful. I thought things through. I planned for potential problems. That is the difference between us."

"Yeah, you kidnapped them, but did it get you money? No. You failed. You had to kill the prime minister, and the American general was rescued in Padova. In the end, you were not successful! Do not preach to me, old man. You had your time. This is my time!"

Saddened, Signore E. paused. "It all sounded great when you told me you were starting up again and that you would find someone rich who would bring ransom money to fund our plans. I was all for it. The blood started coursing through my old veins again. But it was I who found him. I was excited to help plan the mission. Did I make the wrong decision to keep you involved?"

Aware of the boy in the cellar, Signore E. lowered his voice even more and placed his arm around Tomasso's shoulder. "You must understand. You are my nephew and I feel I have to watch over you. I promised my dear brother, may he rest in peace, that I would do that. I hope you accept my guidance."

Pushing the old man's arm off his shoulder, Tomasso replied with disdain, "Do not worry, old man. I will be as successful as you were. Even more so. I am younger, tougher and smarter than you. You will see." He sneered and walked out of the room to join his friends.

Signore E. was angry and frustrated. He punched the wall hard, leaving it damaged. *He could fuck up my life in the blink of an eye. I have to watch his every step and maybe start influencing the others. I know they will follow, especially that cute one Tomasso calls Daisy.*

Eighteen

The smell of body odor permeated the hotel room. Rainee became desperate to get fresh air but would not leave her cell phone. Today was the day the kidnappers had promised to call. The police hoped that now that they were in Florence, the equipment they brought would help pinpoint an address.

Detective Piscitelli arrived at six o'clock with coffees and pastries for Rainee and the three officers playing cards in the corner. The men attacked the food as if they had not eaten in a week.

Rainee had very little appetite. In fact, her stomach was filled with butterflies as she awaited the phone call.

The bags of food were ripped open. Chocolate croissants, cornetto filled with marmalade, pandoro cake, freshly squeezed orange juice, and best of all, caffè and cappuccinos were set out on the table that held the television.

"I think you should eat something, Signora Allen." Detective Piscitelli opened his arms to display the selection of food.

"Please, call me Rainee. Frankly, Detective, I don't think I could keep anything down. I'm quite nervous."

"I understand, Signora... um, I mean, Rainee. Would you prefer tea? I understand the English love their tea."

Rainee managed a weak smile. "I'm American. My husband is English. Well, South American, really. But that's a long story," Her face reddened. "I'm sorry. I tend to rattle on when I'm nervous. Bad habit."

"Not to worry, Rainee. How old is your bambina?"

It was obvious that the detective was trying to get her mind off the cell phone that sat in the middle of the room.

"Jana is five. Or, as she would tell you, five and a half. Do you have children, Detective?"

"Please, call me Fabrizio. And si, I have five children."

"Oh my! I find it difficult keeping up with one five year old."

"Oh, for me it is easy. I am never home."

They both laughed.

"No, I am joking with you. They range in age from eighteen down to nine. When the youngest was born, the older children helped. My wife is very strict and keeps them all in line. Now, can I pour you some caffé?"

"Yes, thank you." Rainee appreciated him introducing some humor to diffuse the tension that hung in the air like London's fog.

She managed to swallow a bite of pandoro cake and wash it down with coffee. The coffee was strong but went down smoothly. Even though it was caffeinated, her butterflies, ironically, seemed to subside.

"Fabrizio, what happened to the Interpol agents? Why didn't they follow us? I expected to see Agent Harrington here."

"Interpol takes over and takes credit only after we police do our job," he said with disdain.

To Rainee this sounded as familiar as the police versus the FBI in America. It always appeared they had contempt for each other's jurisdictions.

Despite expecting it, the ringing of the cell phone startled everybody. Seconds later, everyone was in their positions.

Rainee approached the phone in what felt like slow motion. With a nod from Fabrizio, she lifted it to her ear and pressed the answer button. Her voice sounded wobbly. "Hello."

"Ciao, lady."

"Is... is... Joshua all right? Can I speak to him? Please?" Rainee's knees were shaky. One of the officers slipped a chair under her just in time.

"Do not take me for a fool. I know the polizia are listening. We do not have much time."

"Please, I have to explain something first. I did get in touch with Joshua's father and he insisted on flying out to move the money personally. But for him to liquidate that much money will take a couple of days."

"No. No. *Questo è inaccettabile!*"

Rainee heard him hit something hard.

"Please, please hear me out. He lands here in Rome this morning." Even though they were in Florence already, the kidnappers had no way of knowing that. She looked at Fabrizio, who approved with a nod. "He has agreed to the money. He just needs to go to the bank and work it out. Because it is so much money and you want it in Euros, it will take a day, or maybe two at the most."

"*Vaffanculo.*" He hung up.

Rainee was stunned at his reaction. She held her hands up as if to say; what just happened?

Fabrizio gently said, "They will call back. Do not worry, Rainee. You did great. Really. They will not give up the money."

He turned to his men, "Did you get it?"

"No, not enough time."

"*Dannazione*!" Fabrizio swore, then uttered a few more profanities, but kept them under his breath.

The phone rang again.

This time Rainee picked it up quickly. "Listen you son of a bitch, if you hurt Joshua, there will be no place on this planet where you can hide from me. I will hunt you and your compadres down and kill you myself. Do not underestimate me. If Nazis couldn't stop me six years ago, you small time thugs can't either. *Capito*?"

There was a pause. Then a click. Mickey Mouse hung up again.
Rainee sighed, "What have I done?"
She looked at the men in the room.
They were all staring at her with their mouths open.

Nineteen

"Tomasso! Where are you?" yelled one of the men excitedly. "Tomasso!"

"Here I am. What is the matter?" He was still incensed from the phone call.

The man entered the kitchen with a laptop. "Merda! Look at this! I found this on our little friend's Facebook page. There are many people who are telling him they are sorry for his padre's accident! Some even say they hope he lives! Can you imagine this?"

"*Fanculo!*" yelled Tomasso as he read some of the posts. "How is this possible? Did it just happen?"

He did an internet search with the words Richard Greenberg and accident. The search yielded numerous links. He clicked on one and read the story, his face reddening by the minute. "What the fuck are we going to do?"

He wandered around the room, stomping his feet and hitting any inanimate object he came across. Thinking. Pacing. Fuming.

The door burst open and slammed the wall with a loud bang.

Joshua awoke with a start.

"Did you know about your padre?" screamed Tomasso. "How long have you known?"

"My father? What? What are you talking about?" asked Joshua. "What about my father? Did something happen to him?"

Tomasso glared at him. "Did something happen to him? Did something happen to him? Si, something happened to him! And you better not have known about this!" Tomasso punched the door, leaving a large dent.

"What happened? Is he all right?" Joshua pleaded, "Please tell me!"

"He is in a hospital in California, which means that your Rainee Allen has been playing with me, that bitch! She is pretending he is on his way to deliver the money. *Dannazione!* Well, this is no game. She will see! Either she delivers exactly the amount we demanded, or I will kill you."

He stomped out of the room, slammed the door behind him and yelled. "*Fanculo, cagna!* You will be sorry! You will see!"

Joshua was stunned. Time seemed to stand still. *Dad! Oh my God, Dad! In a hospital? Is it true? What happened? How did it happen? What condition is he in? Is he going to die? And what will become of me? How will he get the money to them?*

Shit, Rainee must be panicked about me. I never showed up and no word. God, she must be so worried! I wonder if she knows about Dad.

Dazed for a few seconds, Joshua buried his face in his hands and sobbed uncontrollably. Tears flowed down his cheeks. He was more tired than he ever remembered. He imagined it was because he was experiencing both deep sadness and panic.

Yelling in the next room snapped him back to reality. His present awful reality.

Then the sound of keys unlocking the door made him brace for more cruelty as it slowly opened. It was Daisy.

Because his eyes were red and swollen, Joshua quickly looked away. His cheeks streaked with tears.

She approached the bed. "I cannot believe this!" she whispered. "I heard about your padre. Sorry. I do not know what will happen now. Will we still be able to get the money?" she wondered aloud, and immediately regretted it.

Joshua said nothing. He was profoundly sad and worried about his father and his own future.

Unable to restrain them in front of Daisy, his tears kept falling. It embarrassed him, yet he could not stop.

Though not his intention, it definitely had an effect on her. It was not long before she tried to comfort him.

She touched his arm awkwardly, then put her hand on his, patting it gently. She kept repeating, "Shhhhh, shhhhh," not knowing what else to say.

Her gesture was not lost on Joshua. He appreciated her unexpected kindness and compassion. His crying subsided.

Daisy's hand lingered, and it surprised them both. This hardened woman had a soft, nurturing side that came out unexpectedly.

He looked up at her.

Her mahogany brown eyes met his and lingered for a moment.

She raised her hand to caress his face but withdrew it swiftly. It struck her as inappropriate and she regained her composure as she pulled away. The moment ended almost as quickly as it started.

She felt conflicted. Daisy knew it was important to be as unattached as possible with their captive. On the other hand, she did feel some sympathy for this young, innocent man who seemed so out of place in this situation. And perhaps she was a little bit attracted to him.

Daisy had seen his license and knew they were only a year apart. *We must have some things in common. Does he like the same music I like? Games? Hobbies? But he is a brilliant young man with degrees. He is cultured and was brought up with money. Who am I? A nobody. A rebel. A kidnapper!*

Joshua interrupted her thoughts. "Do you know what happened to my father?"

She nodded. "Si, but I know very little. One of our men was on Facebook when he decided to look up your page just for fun. He did and found many messages expressing sorrow and concern and wishing your padre well. The best we can tell is that he had a car accident and he is in the hospital. That is all we know. I am sorry."

Joshua's eyes welled up again and he tried hard not to let them spill over. *I can't believe you're in the hospital, Dad!*

His chin began to quiver. The other ominous thought crept back into his consciousness again. *What will happen to me now that they know my dad won't be able to pay a ransom?*

He was as scared as he had ever been.

He looked at her. "Do you know what they will do with me now?"

"No. I do not. No one knows what to do. We will talk with the original group, whose house we are in. They will know what to do."

She looked a little scared herself, and that unsettled Joshua's nerves even more.

Will they really kill me or was the threat just leverage for them? Are the police on their trail? How do I let the police or Rainee know where I am now? Will they move me again?

He decided to see if he could somehow get Daisy to tell him where they were in case he ever had the opportunity to speak to them.

Joshua wanted her to look him in the eyes again. His eyes expressed fear. He hoped this would play on her sympathies. "Do you know what their plans were before they read about my father? Were they planning on killing me even if they got the money?"

Daisy sighed, "No, I do not think they would do that. I do not think they ever really planned on that. I know I should not say anything to you, but frankly, I am getting sick of Toma— I mean, Mickey Mouse's mean way with me. I hate him!"

Joshua noted her mistake. It sounded like she was going to say Thomas, or a name close to that.

"You know, he was not always like that." She looked away. "He was charming, even nice. We were even a couple for a while. That is how he got me to go along with this idea. Kidnap a rich kid and demand ransom. Okay, it is not— how do you say?— original, that's it. It is not original, but we all thought it could work. God, how I would love to just get away from here!

I think, sometimes, about how we met and what a great relationship we had at the beginning. As I said, he was even charming. I know that seems funny now, after you have seen how terrible he can be, but he really was nice a long time ago." She smiled.

Joshua waited a moment, then asked, "How did you meet him. And how did he get you to join this group?"

"We met at a party in Barra, a city not far from Napoli. I lived there with my mother and my sister. He was so nice to me at the party that I said I would go on a date with him. My mother did not like him though." She laughed. "She said he looked like a *fuorilegge*, a— oh, how you say?— a criminal or outlaw. I thought he was very good-looking, even though he had a beard and tattoos. I was not used to seeing men like that in my town.

Believe it or not, I was a good girl. My father died when I was six years old. We practically lived in the church after that. My mother made us go to church every day. Every day! I hated it, but what can you do when your mother takes your hand and pulls you to it?" She stopped for moment. "But I am speaking too much. You do not care about my young life. I will stop."

"No. Please go on. I'd really like to know," Joshua said earnestly. He was interested and besides, the more he knew, the better. Maybe something she said would be useful. *I do feel for her, but I have to remember that she took part in kidnapping me.*

"Well, my mother was very strict with my sister and me. She would hardly ever let us go to dances or parties, even though we were of legal age. She was always afraid something would happen to us, like we would meet a man. Can you imagine how horrible that would be?" She started laughing, and that's when Joshua noticed how pretty she was. When she laughed, her eyes crinkled at the corners, and a dimple appeared in both cheeks.

"When I met him at that party, I thought he was very handsome. We talked a little at the party, and then we started to go out. At first, it was fun, but then he started bringing me to his friends' houses. Sometimes it was scary. They were all very political and angry, it seemed."

Joshua nodded. "Go on."

"They went on and on about politics and the government and got together with some older guys, who were members of the original Brigate Rosse. The lucky ones who lived through that era. They spent nights drinking and planning a revival of the organization. I just happened to be there at the right— or wrong— time.

Well, they decided they needed money to start with their plans, so I guess you know the rest. You are the source of that money."

She went on. "I never thought about the man at the end of the plan: you. I was just promised lots of money. I planned to use that to go to America. I always wanted to see New York. That was my plan." Her head tipped down. "I now know I was wrong to go after dirty money."

Joshua saw an opening to try to get closer. He put his hand over hers. "Yeah. I understand. You needed to get away. Your boyfriend treats you horribly. He's a real asshole. I can't believe he hit you. You seem like a good person."

"I do not think you really think so, especially since I am part of this group. The truth is, I thought this would be easy— make the money exchange and just leave— but it is turning into a mess. A real mess. I am scared now because I am not sure what will happen, or how it will turn out for me. I am not even sure that we will get the money. And even if we do, will I get my share? I do not trust Tomasso anymore."

She suddenly realized she used his real name. *Who cares? Fuck him*, she thought. "We were so close to the money, and now the whole thing seems like its falling apart. I am worried... for both of us." Her voice cracked. "I am through being treated like a dog! He cannot treat me like this!"

He tentatively put his hand on her shoulder, expecting a sudden rejection, but it did not come. In fact, Daisy leaned into him.

Joshua found himself consoling her. He put his arm around her shoulder and pulled her closer to him. She did not resist.

"You know, it seems like I hooked myself to a bunch of idiots. I cannot believe I did this. They are screwing up and fighting with each other at every turn. Even the new ransom idea is stupid, but maybe a little funny." She released a small chuckle.

Joshua looked up. "Funny?"

Feeling it was safe to tell him what the plan was, Daisy said, "Idiots! They are planning on dressing up in costumes and making the exchange for you at the Romeo and Juliet Festival this week! I think that is funny, do you? They sent Giorgio, the short, balding one, to Verona to buy costumes for all of us!"

She started laughing. "Can you believe it? He will have us all dress up in costumes. Even you! You will be Romeo." Her nervous laughter intensified. "There will be many people there, all dressed in costumes with masks. Many Romeos. Many Juliets. We will be lost in the crowd."

After a moment, Joshua pushed more conversation to win her trust. "Actually, I like the story of Romeo and Juliet. Two people from different worlds who fall in love."

He looked at her and grinned.

She smiled back.

He said, "I played Romeo years ago in high school. It took me a long time to learn those lines."

That made Daisy laugh.

"Is the festival here?" he asked.

"It is not far. Each year it is held in Montecchio Maggiore, at the Romeo and Juliet castle, called Via Castello Bella Guardia. The two castles there supposedly inspired the story."

She breathed deeply. "It is really beautiful there. There are medieval dances, dueling, falconry shows and food. Lots of food. I even worked there when I was younger. You see, I grew up around—"

Noise outside the door broke the spell. Daisy stopped talking and quickly stood up, away from the bed.

Joshua was instantly brought back to his previous state of fear.

She looked at him and put her finger up to her lips.

Twenty

Rainee felt desperate and fearful. "My God, what have I done? I don't know what came over me. Why did I say that? Will they call back? Fabrizio, will they call back?"

Fabrizio took the phone from Rainee's shaking hands. He guided her to a chair, placed his hands on her shoulders, and gently pressed her to sit. The detective looked at his tech team to see if they traced the call.

They shook their heads.

He took a deep breath and picked up a chair to place in front of Rainee. He quietly sat down, faced her, and thought for a moment before he spoke. He did not want to dishearten her any more than she already was. "Do not be hard on yourself. You were like a warrior. Like a lioness protecting her cub. A mother protecting her child. You spoke in anger, but that was from the heart. The kidnappers must now know how invested you are in the boy.

They will call back, Rainee. There is no question in my mind. They want the money, and for that reason, they will not hurt him."

Rainee lifted her eyes. Her shaking had subsided. "How can you know that?"

"Because it is obvious to them that you are their link to Joshua and his family's money. If they did not believe it before, they do now." He exhaled. "Now listen carefully, Rainee. The next time the phone rings— and it will ring— I want you to take charge of the conversation. Ask firmly— do not demand— ask to speak to Joshua. We need to find out where they are. You are a writer. Get creative. Send hints to get him to hint back. Use incorrect names, places, memories. He will pick up on it. He is a smart boy."

"He's a frightened boy."

"Just insist on hearing his voice. You took over that last conversation. You can do it again."

Just then, the phone rang and Rainee jumped.

"Breathe, Rainee. You can do this." He handed her the cell phone.

"This is Rainee."

To her surprise, it was Joshua's quivering voice at the end of the phone. "It's me, Rainee."

"Joshua! Are you okay?"

"I'm a mess. I just heard about Dad. What happened?"

"He was on his way to bring the ransom money. He must've been out of his mind with worry. His... his Ferrari was hit."

"His Ferrari? You mean his—"

"That's right. The red Ferrari. He was getting on Highway 484... you know how dangerous that ramp is."

"484? What the—"

"Sure, the same route you took every day to... Berkeley." *Please*, she thought. *Please pick up on the clues.*

There was a slight pause. Then Joshua said, "Yeah, sure. I know that entrance."

Using the same pretense, Joshua asked, "Do you know which house he was coming from?"

Rainee faltered, "Which house?"

"Oh, I guess it doesn't really matter. There are two... two households, both are alike in dignity," responded Joshua. That sentence triggered a distant memory, but Rainee thought better of asking what he meant.

There was a sound of a scuffle and men arguing.

The voice of Mickey Mouse came on. He was breathing heavily. "Enough, Signora. We want our money. Now we know you lied to us. His padre is in the hospital. He is not headed to Roma with the money. So how are you going to get us the five million Euros? No more stalling."

"Sir, I will get the money. I promise. What... what is your name? What do I call you?"

"Call me Mickey Mouse. I will call back in four hours. I will then tell you exactly how and when you will get the money to us. Ciao." Click.

Fabrizio looked at the tech.

The man shook his head. "Too short. Came close though."

"*Dannazione!*" The men were huddled in the corner speaking to each other.

Rainee said, "I've got it!"

The men continued their discussion.

Rainee raised her voice. "I said, I've got it!"

The detectives' discussion came to a dead stop. Fabrizio said, "What is it, Rainee?"

"Let me double-check something. Hand me your laptop." She typed in several sentences. "Yes! That's it. Joshua took my hints and gave us an answer.

He quoted from *Romeo and Juliet*. When we planned to meet in Venice, he told me he liked Shakespeare's *Merchant of Venice* and had to read several of his plays. He said he loved *Romeo and Juliet* and even played Romeo in high school." She caught her breath. "It took me a moment. I knew it sounded familiar. I just couldn't put it together." She pointed at the screen. "Look."

Rainee turned the laptop to reveal the result of her internet search. It read, *Two households, both alike in dignity*.

"Si, but how does that help? I do not understand."

"Continue reading. It's from Romeo and Juliet." she said.

Two households, both alike in dignity, In fair Verona, where we lay our scene.

The detectives spoke over each other with confused looks on their faces. All but Fabrizio. "Fair Verona! They are in Verona!"

Rainee smiled and nodded her head. "Smart boy, my son."

Twenty-One

Ricky slowly opened his eyes to the blaring lights in his hospital room. The sound of an alarm going off jerked him into consciousness. A nurse came over to his bed and pushed some buttons on the machine hooked up to a pole. There was a jungle of poles around his bed, with liquids slowly dripping into his body.

The nurse looked down at him and smiled warmly. "Good morning, Mr. Greenberg." She took his vitals.

Ricky tried to shake off the haze in his head. "Morning?" His mouth was dry. "What time is it? How long have I been out?"

"Two days. Your vitals look good. The doctor is making his rounds. He'll be in shortly."

"Wait! Where's my wife?"

"She's been by your bedside since they brought you in. I think they said she was going down to the cafeteria. One of the nurses convinced her to eat something to keep up her strength. She gave the desk her cell phone number. We can let her know you're awake now."

"What about Joshua?"

"Who?"

"My son, Joshua. In Italy. They kidnapped him. What about Joshua?"

"Oh, you must've been dreaming. You've been on some very heavy drugs. They can sometimes cause hallucinations or strange dreams."

"No, no, it's true. Please, get my wife. Get her now. I have to find out about my son." He tried to push his body upright.

The nurse quickly put her hands on the front of his shoulders and pressed him back down. "Now, now, Mr. Greenberg. You need to calm down. You don't want to pull out any of your IVs do you? I can give you a sedative to help calm you."

"No! Don't! Please, just get me my wife. Please."

"Certainly, sir. Just promise me you won't try to get up."

Ricky nodded weakly.

The nurse left.

Ricky said a silent prayer that his son was still alive as tears rolled down his cheeks.

It was not long before Deborah rushed into the room. Careful not to hurt him, she clutched him in a tight hug. "Oh, Ricky darling. You're going to be all right. Thank God, you're going to be fine." She was crying. Her words muffled as she sobbed into his hospital gown.

"Deb, tell me about Josh. What's happened?"

Deborah shook her head and wiped away her tears.

The look on her face frightened Ricky. He grabbed her shoulders. "What? What's happened? Is he okay?"

"Sweetheart, I need you to calm down. You just had major surgery."

"Tell me!"

"There is no change. The kidnappers still have him. They're insisting on the money. Rainee says the police don't think they will hurt him because they want the money. They found out about your accident."

"How?"

"Social media. Someone leaked it from the hospital. Rainee said they gave her only one day to come up with the money."

"Okay, I'll take the company jet."

She looked at him like he was crazy. "Darling, you're not going anywhere. You can't bend your leg. Not if you ever want to walk again. Have you looked at yourself?"

Ricky removed the sheets and looked at his right leg in horror. "Oh my God, what is this? What are those things?"

"Steel rods. They are in your bones, so you can heal. Your leg has to remain immobilized for six weeks, darling."

"Immobilized? I have to get to Josh. We need to get the money to Rainee."

Deborah took his hand. "We will. Now that you're awake, we will."

He shook his head and looked away.

Deborah said, "Ricky, look at me. Please. Look at me."

He reluctantly faced her.

"He'll be fine. Rainee will see to that. I spoke with her and she's been in communication with Josh. They let her speak to him. Our brilliant son sent her clues about where they are. They moved their operation to Verona. Rainee said the Italian police believe that's where the exchange will happen."

"But how could they know that?"

"Apparently, this group is a faction of the Red Brigade. It's who captured the American General Dozier back in the early eighties. Remember that?"

"Vaguely."

"Verona may be where the base of their operations is. At least, that's what the police suspect. So it's likely that they won't be moving again. The police think Joshua will be safe as long as they get the money."

"I want to speak with Rainee."

Deborah looked at her watch. "Okay, it's eight hours ahead. So let's see... it's 4:50 p.m. there. Rainee bought a dedicated cell phone to keep in touch with us." She fished around in her purse and pulled out her phone. She dialed, then handed the phone to her husband.

The phone rang twice.

It was a sweet, familiar voice from his past. "Hello, Deborah?"

"No, Rainee. It's me... Ricky."

Twenty-Two

"You better pray that your lady friend gets us the money, stupid boy! I am not playing her games anymore. If we do not get it in twenty-four hours, then you are dead! Dead!" Tomasso yelled. He spat on the floor to further emphasize his domination over Joshua, then turned swiftly and left.

Daisy took Joshua's arm roughly and led him back to his basement cell. "Get back in there!" she yelled, trying to make herself seem as tough as possible.

They entered the room and she immediately let go of his arm. "Oh, what are we going to do? She better be able to get the money, because Tomasso is not playing. I hope she knows that."

Joshua hoped she knew it too. Daisy looked at him for several seconds as if pondering something important. Then she whispered, "Good night," and left the room.

Joshua did not hear the metallic sound of a key turning in the lock after she closed the door. *Was that intentional?*

He waited a few moments, then approached the door. He quietly turned the doorknob and pushed.

Oh my God. It's open! He started breathing rapidly. *I've just been given a break. Daisy is telling me I should try to escape. This is so dangerous. No, I have to escape.* Joshua trembled with fear.

Quietly, he walked out of his tiny room. A little light spilled out with him. He shivered and peered into the cold, dark cellar. Rough, hand-made wooden shelving, sagging with age, caught his attention. Some odds and ends were deposited on it: an old rusted paint can, some nails, a few screws, an old rag and a yardstick hanging on a nail.

In the thin stream of light something shiny caught his attention. There, sticking out from behind the jar of nails, was a screwdriver. For the first time in several days, Joshua felt a glimmer of hope. He grabbed the tool and brought it back into his room, taking care to close the door with barely a click. He slipped the tool under the mattress.

How would I use it? I may need it to protect myself. And to protect Daisy. I can't watch her get hit again. But he questioned whether he could actually use it as a weapon. He didn't think he had it in him to stab someone. Or did he? Thoughts of childhood fights flooded his mind. He had had only two fights in his life. One on the playground in elementary school, and the other a few years later, around the corner from where he lived. Both were started by bullies.

Joshua remembered being punched in the face multiple times by one opponent, while he could only muster enough aggression to aim for his adversary's stomach.

But this was a very different situation. His very life might depend on his willingness to use a screwdriver as a weapon. The very thought of plunging the tool into another person frightened him nearly as much as facing an unknown outcome to his captivity.

But they say you never know what you're capable of doing in a fight or flight situation, until you are in one. I guess I'll have to wait and see what my choice will be.

He was not a violent kid and certainly not a violent adult. In fact, he had decided to devote his life to resolving conflict. To help find alternative ways to solve problems between people, and here he was nearing the end of his formal education in Conflict Resolution. He needed to put some of those lessons to use. *But can I reason with my captors using logic and the emotional awareness tools I've learned? How can I manage to establish a realistic communication process that can help me?*

He lay on the mattress racked with both terror and hope for the first time since he was abducted. *Okay, I need to plan how to get out of here. This might be my only chance, so tonight it is.*

He glanced at his watch and noted the time. It was nearly ten o'clock. He could still hear voices and footsteps from the floor above. He just could not take this anymore. He started to develop a plan.

He would wait until everyone upstairs was asleep and prayed no one would stand guard.

Twenty-Three

"Ricky. Oh, Ricky. It's so good to hear your voice!"

"Yeah, yours too."

"Last I heard you were totally out of it. How do you feel?"

"Like I got hit by a truck." He laughed, and it hurt him everywhere. "Oh right, I did."

"Yes, Deborah told me about your leg. But you're alive. Thank God for that."

"Yeah." There was silence. They both were thinking of what the alternative could have been. Ricky broke the silence. "Joshua?"

"Let me bring you up to date."

Rainee explained how Joshua dropped clues with the last call from the kidnappers. She said she was still with the police, they were on the road and it would take about two and a half hours to reach Verona. When the next call came through, she would say that the police would put up the money because they knew he would reimburse the government. Once the exchange location was determined, the police would set up a rescue scenario. She had her doubts about the logistics, but she did believe Detective Fabrizio Piscitelli to be a good detective, so she agreed.

"Ricky," her voice softened. "That Joshua— I can't tell you. I mean, he's such a—" She couldn't find the words. Rainee's lower lip quivered. She fought back her tears because she wanted to stay strong for Ricky.

"I know, Rainee. I know. He's pretty special."

"You and Deborah did an outstanding job bringing him up. I can't wait to finally sit quietly and talk with him. Without all this drama."

"I thought you liked drama. You know, as a writer. I guess now you have new material for your next novel."

"Nope. Not this time. Too personal."

They both laughed.

For Rainee, the years melted away, just hearing his familiar voice. The warmth of their earlier friendship comforted her. Despite the situation, she felt their kinship, like all the years, had never passed.

"Ricky, I'm going to bring Joshua home to you. I promise I won't let anything happen to him."

"I know you will, Rain. I'm counting on you."

She could hear a nurse in the background. She caught every other word. Then there was a man's voice.

Ricky was arguing with him. Then his weary voice came back on the line. "Sorry, Rainee, the doctors are insisting they want to examine me. I'll hand you over to Deborah. Be careful. Be safe. We'll talk again soon."

Deborah's voice sounded worried. "Rainee, he can be so stubborn."

Rainee laughed. "But he's going to be all right. He will, won't he?"

"The doctors say he'll make a full recovery. That is, if he doesn't jump out of bed and pull out all these IVs. He wants to be there. For Josh. For you. He feels so helpless, and nothing I say will deter him. At least now, he can have his lawyer arrange for the ransom. In fact, the lawyer is on his way to the hospital right now to get the ball rolling."

Rainee sighed. "Oh good. That's a relief."

"I'm glad you're there for Josh. Oh my God, if anything happens to that boy— I just can't—" Deborah choked up.

Rainee bit her lower lip. She said with resolve, "Nothing will happen to him, Deborah. I will do whatever it takes to bring him home to Ricky and you. It will be all right. I promise."

Rainee asked Deborah to keep her informed of Ricky's recovery, then closed the cell phone.

The van turned off the highway and onto the road to Verona.

Twenty-Four

Joshua listened intently for any noises upstairs that might indicate that people were still awake. He heard none.

A glance at his watch told him that it was after midnight. The house seemed still. It felt like now was as good a time as any to escape. He got up to relieve himself in the bucket they had placed in his room. He remembered how he felt about it when he arrived at the house, disgusted at the thought of using it. Now, he was happy it was in the room.

Joshua reached under the mattress and retrieved the screwdriver. He reached for his jacket and shoes. Then he walked the three steps to the door, turned the door handle and stepped out as quietly as possible. Aware that the old wooden stairs creaked, he tip-toed slowly up the stairs, his feet close to the edge. He took two at a time and was rewarded for his care. No sound. When he got to the top step, he discovered a problem he had not anticipated.

The door into the living area was locked.

He put the screwdriver to work but found it was not as easy as he had hoped. Even though he turned it in both directions and at various depths, it would not unlock. Joshua was grateful it was not a deadbolt, which would make it nearly impossible to open. It was an old door with the kind of lock that had a spring-loaded latch, which should be easy to push in with the screwdriver.

Now, if I can only manage to... Finally he heard a subtle click and the lock gave way to freedom.

There were men sleeping on chairs and splayed out on the floor. He moved as quietly as he could. He crossed the living room toward the front door. Opening this door posed no challenges. He turned the lock slowly and pulled open the door with barely a sound.

He pocketed the tool and slipped into the cool air. *Where to go?* All he knew was to get away from the house, and as fast as possible.

Quickly and quietly he walked toward the dirt road. When he reached it, he turned left and started running. The gravel and small stones hurt his feet. They produced several cuts that started bleeding but somehow it felt wonderful.

The feeling was overwhelming.

Several hundred feet down the road he put his shoes on and quickly tied them. He started to think about his mother. *Mom will cry when she hears the news. Both moms will.* Elated, he started running as fast as he could.

After several minutes Joshua started to slow down and walk. He was breathless. It was a moonless night and dark, but with just enough starlight to make out the road.

No cars passed, and the road seemed to go on forever, but that did not matter to the escapee, who seemed to be floating on a cloud, rather than walking on dirt and gravel. His walk was fueled by the potent mixture of adrenaline and excitement.

After about fifteen minutes, he settled into a relaxed, determined pace. In the distance, headlights from a car appeared. Joshua kept his stride. As the car neared, he left the road, crossed a small grassy area and crouched down behind a tractor parked at the edge of a building site. In the distance, a dog started barking.

The car passed.

Joshua waited until the tail lights were far in the distance, then stood up and walked back to the road.

After several minutes, another vehicle approached. Joshua hid behind some tall bushes at the side of the road.

Again, the car passed uneventfully.

Twenty-Five

Verona— home of Shakespeare's *Romeo and Juliet*, *The Two Gentlemen of Verona*, and *The Taming of the Shrew*. It was also the original base of the infamous Red Brigade and where American General Dozier was kidnapped.

Sometime after midnight, Rainee and the police entered their new temporary headquarters in a private house in Verona. It was small with only two bedrooms and one bathroom and was located on a sparsely-settled street where homes were hundreds of feet apart.

The house appeared to have been unoccupied for quite a while. Dust had settled everywhere, along with dead cockroaches. Rainee dusted off a chair and sat at the kitchen table. On it were two souvenir coffee cups. She noted the imprint of red lipstick on one of them. An ashtray overflowed with cigarette butts, a crumbled piece of paper, and two squashed bugs. Rainee took out a tissue and cleaned off the table top. The detectives did not seem to notice the dirt and were busy guzzling down espressos and setting up computers.

Rainee borrowed a laptop again to search for more information regarding the Red Brigade and all the factions that had broken off from them. She wanted to know who she was dealing with and how she could prepare. The phone would ring in the morning, and she wanted to be ready. She wanted to be able to take control of the situation and of the man who called himself Mickey Mouse. But how?

The research she found was frightening. The Red Brigade was considered a left-wing paramilitary organization. It was responsible for numerous violent acts, including assassinations, kidnappings and robberies during the 1970s and early 1980s.

They had kidnapped Italian Prime Minister Aldo Moro on March 16, 1978 and then killed him after fifty-four days of captivity.

Rainee gasped and continued reading.

In 1980, the Italian police detained twelve thousand far-left militants. Approximately three hundred fled to France and nearly two hundred to South America. Another hundred or so went into hiding in Europe. Most of the leaders who were arrested either retracted their doctrine or collaborated with investigators in the capture of other Red Brigade members in exchange for reducing their prison sentences.

Rainee wondered if there were any pictures of their leaders. She switched to search images. The red flag of the Brigate Rosse with a five-pointed star surrounded by a circle popped up throughout most images. There were faded black and white images of militant, long-haired, beret-wearing men and women posed in groups, smoking and smiling. Fists were poised defiantly in the air. Pictures of people being led to jail, along with a few color images, filled the screen. She scanned through the pictures.

Rainee's eyes hesitated on one photograph. She was not sure what it was about the teenage boy's face that gave her a feeling of uncertainty. A cigarette dangled from his mouth and he was holding a flag, smiling the proud smile of a dissident defying the government. There was something familiar about him, perhaps his eyes. But she could not determine what or why.

She turned to one of the police. "Can you show me how to make these pictures bigger and clearer?"

He complied, and she returned her attention to the face that seemed to stand out from the crowd. She was perplexed. Why was the young boy's face familiar?

Again, she turned to the police. "Can you find out who this boy is? There's something familiar about him. I'm not sure what."

"Signora, that was a long time ago. I'm not sure we would be able to do that."

"Then how about sending a copy to Interpol? Try. Per favore."

The detective looked down at his shoes and began to wave his hands in dispute.

That was not good enough for Rainee, so she turned to Fabrizio. "I can't be positive whether this means anything. But I have a gut feeling. And I learned a long time ago not to ignore these hunches. Please, Fabrizio."

"I cannot," he replied, then went to pour himself a cup of coffee.

His dismissal surprised her. For a moment she wondered why, but then returned to the picture, deeply rooting the face in her brain. There was just something about that face.

She would not be deterred. She found the business card Agent Roger Harrington from Interpol had handed her in Rome and sent a request via email to him with the picture attached.

I certainly don't need Fabrizio's permission.

Twenty-Six

Joshua walked for another hour.

The dark countryside offered the occasional farmhouse, and animals reacted to his sudden appearance with barking, mooing or neighing. The noise sometimes startled him, but at this hour of the morning, he felt lucky it was only that.

There were no street signs or house numbers. He wondered how the post office delivered their mail?

Cars still passed occasionally, and he started to feel more confident. He moved off the road only as they were passing him. How great it would be to see everyone again!

His thoughts about Daisy went back and forth. For one thing, he feared for her safety. In another few hours, all hell would break loose in the farmhouse, and she would most certainly bear the brunt of Tomasso's anger.

But she *was* part of the plot to kidnap and possibly kill him.

Still, there was something he liked about her. She did regret joining the band of criminals, after all. She even left his door unlocked. *And she has an appealing softness.*

Still, she did help kidnap him in the first place.

Another set of headlights passed.

Joshua was so lost in his concern, he kept walking. He barely noticed the sound of tires sliding on the gravel behind him. The car turned quickly and hurtled toward him, kicking up gravel and a cloud of dirt behind it.

Shit! Joshua barely had time to react. He was in serious trouble. He started running as fast as he could down the road in the same direction he'd been walking.

The car was upon him in seconds.

He turned and started running across a field that had been recently plowed.

As he ran, he reached into his jacket pocket and pulled out the screwdriver. His fist tightly gripped it.

As the car slowed to navigate the bumpy terrain, he paced his stride so his feet landed atop each furrow.

Behind him, the car door opened.

He glanced back to see how close the other man was. He tightened his hold on the screwdriver.

His pursuer was overtaking him.

Joshua tried to increase his speed and—

His world turned upside down.

He was face down in the dirt.

A large man fell on him, knocking the breath out of his body.

Joshua lost his hold on the screwdriver, and the man wrapped one strong arm around his neck from behind.

Joshua struggled, but the pressure on his neck was too much.

Darkness enveloped him.

Giorgio yelled, "Tomasso! Tomasso! Wake up!"

Lights came on and people slowly stirred.

A moment later, Tomasso entered the living room rubbing his eyes, followed by other yawning members of the group.

Tomasso stared in disbelief.

The captive, who was supposed to be locked in the basement room, was there before him. He was just regaining consciousness.

And Giorgio was holding him upright.

Giorgio grinned. “Look who I found strolling down the road! After I picked up the costumes you wanted, I met up with a couple of my friends in town and went to a bar for drinks. I was on my way back when I saw this asshole ambling down the road, like he had all the time in the world.”

Tomasso’s eyes widened. “What the fuck was he doing outside? How the hell did he escape?” He stared at everyone in the room.

They all looked at him incredulously.

“Who did this?” He scanned the tired group. “Merda, only one person is not here.” Tomasso yelled, “Giorgio, go wake up Daisy! That puttana will pay for this!”

He turned to two other men. “Niccolo, Stefano, hold this piece of shit. He thinks we are just fooling around. Well, it is time to show him we are serious.”

The two men each held an arm and Tomasso stepped up to Joshua, who was now fully cognizant. “You will now see that this is not a game, little rich boy.”

Joshua struggled to loosen the grip of the two men, but it was no use. They were much too strong for him.

The first punch to his abdomen almost knocked him out. Joshua’s legs started to fold under him.

Tomasso shook his head. “Not so fast! This will last a while and I am going to enjoy it! Hold him up!”

The second swing connected with Joshua’s left eye.

It felt as if the eye was driven out of its socket. He could no longer see through it. Warm blood coated his cheek.

“You want to run away, rich boy? You think this is a game? Like that bitch Rainee Allen. She thinks this is a game, too. Well, I think both of you will see who is playing a game and who is not! And while we are having this enjoyable, little talk, tell me, who is this Rainee Allen?”

Joshua tasted blood as it dripped down his face and into his mouth. He hesitated, then said, “Rainee Allen? She’s a teacher from my school. She came for the conference.”

“You are lying! Who is she, this liaison? I know she is not police. Tell me! I want to hear it from your own mouth.”

"She is no one. Leave her out of it."

Tomasso punched him in the gut again. "She is already involved, rich boy. She is our connection to your papa's money. Say it. I want to hear you say it."

Again, Tomasso punched Joshua, and his legs buckled. He would have fallen had it not been for the two men holding him up.

"She is... my mother." Joshua felt nauseous. "I need to vomit."

"You lie again. Your Facebook page says that someone named Deborah is your mother." Tomasso had lost all patience with Joshua. He took a threatening stance over the young man and screamed, "Tell me!"

Joshua began to cry. "Deborah is my step-mom. Rainee is my biological mother. She gave me up for adoption when I was born."

Tomasso nodded to the two men, and they let Joshua drop to his knees.

He held his abdomen from the pain and sobbed.

Tomasso nodded his head. He took the one he called Donald Duck aside and whispered instructions to him.

Donald Duck bobbed his head in agreement, then swiftly left the house. There was the sound of tires on gravel as the man drove off into the distance.

Tomasso inspected his bleeding knuckles, then held them down in front of Joshua's face. "Look at what you did to my hands, rich boy."

The two men picked Joshua up and held his full weight, for he had no strength left. Joshua felt he might not be able to take another punch. He was right.

A hard punch hit his nose and he lost consciousness. The men holding him had no choice but to let his body slump to the floor. Blood gushed as if the punch had released a pressure valve.

Tomasso said, "Prop him up. I want to take a picture of his face to convince his father and that Rainee bitch and the police how serious we are about this. In fact, I think I will send a note along with it. Not only will this continue until he is unrecognizable, I might even start removing body parts."

Stefano protested. "Capo, you said no one would—"

Tomasso whirled. “You would dare defy me?” They were almost nose to nose.

“No. No, Tomasso. Whatever you say.”

Tomasso glared around the room. “Does anyone here defy me?”

No one spoke.

He pointed at Joshua. “I say a picture of that face will ensure us there will be no more fucking delays! Now, Stefano, go find a camera.”

Stefano returned with a Canon small point-and-shoot digital camera. He turned it on and gave it to Tomasso. “I found this in the kitchen. It is your girlfriend’s, no? There is some justice in our using her camera to send a picture of her boyfriend’s bloody face, eh?”

The others nodded and smiled.

“Prop him up so I can get a nice beauty shot! And do not wipe away any of the blood. They will recognize him, I am sure.” As an afterthought, he said, “And post it to his Facebook page. Let the world see what the Red Brigade is capable of.”

Tomasso took several pictures and chose the most convincing one. “When his father sees this— if his father sees it— he will start throwing money at us! Maybe we should raise the ransom!”

All of them started laughing.

“Now, upload this one to the computer in the back and let me know when you are done. I want to write a nice little note to send with it.”

After they were done, Tomasso said, “Clean him up a little. Then take this piece of shit back to the room downstairs. And make goddamn sure the door is locked!”

Someone yanked on Joshua’s arms, then lifted him and carried him toward the cellar door.

Tomasso said, “And clean the floor too. We do not want to upset our host!”

Signore E. came into the room. “Fuck the floor! Tomasso, I can’t believe you let something like this happen. You nearly killed that boy! How would you get the money then? Why did you not have a guard on him?”

"Shut up, old man! I am tired of your constant judgement! There are two doors with two locks! *Two!* How could he have escaped? Where are the keys?" He then shouted, "And where is Daisy?"

Giorgio returned out of breath and without Daisy. "She is gone!"

"That is not possible!" responded Tomasso.

"No, Tomasso! I saw her. She is in the back field, running from the house! She must have gone out the window."

Tomasso leapt over a chair and almost knocked someone over trying to get out the door. He and Giorgio ran around the house.

Daisy was in the distance, running through the field.

It did not take very long for Tomasso to catch up to her. He tackled her. When they stopped rolling, Tomasso was on top.

She was wide-eyed and breathing heavily.

Giorgio caught up to them.

"Stupid whore!" Tomasso slapped her hard. "I cannot believe you let him go! He was our way to real money! A better life for all of us! For you too!"

She was too scared to respond.

He grabbed her arm and yanked her up. "How could you do this?"

The anger in his eyes was a prelude to what would follow.

She said nothing.

He gave no warning as he delivered a crushing punch to her face. It knocked her down. Her lip split, and blood trickled down her face. She lay on the ground as he continued to yell and swear.

"Tomasso! Stop! Take it—" Giorgio started to protest.

"Shut up!"

Tomasso bent down, lifted her onto his shoulder and carried her back through the field.

When the others saw her bleeding profusely as he carried through the front door, they loudly protested.

Tomasso wheeled around and yelled, "She is a traitor! She can no longer be trusted! Any more shit and it will be much worse! That goes for any one of you."

He brought her to her room and shoved her onto the bed.

He barked an order to one of his people. "Nail her window shut. This one in her bedroom and the small bathroom. And make sure they cannot be opened! You!" He pointed to one of his men. "Stand guard by her door."

Tomasso quickly went to the kitchen, grabbed a pad of paper and a pen and started writing a letter to Joshua's father:

Richard Greenberg, as you see from the picture, we have your son. It may look like he is dead, but believe me, he is very much alive and very much in pain. I expect that you would like to keep him alive, but I can assure you of that only if there are NO MORE EXCUSES and NO MORE DELAYS.

We want our money and we want it NOW! If we do not receive it by tomorrow at the drop point we will specify, I will kill your son. But I will not kill him fast. I will take a little piece of him each day until his body gives out. Fingers, toes, arms, legs. He will bleed to death. It will be very painful for him. You probably do not want this to happen, si?

You have the power to stop it. For now, he is in one piece. Send the money and keep it that way!

Tomasso yelled, "Stefano, did you upload the picture yet? I need you to type this into the computer. Now!"

Joshua had come to full consciousness with Tomasso's loud rants. He could only imagine what Daisy suffered at the thug's hand. He felt sick to his stomach.

God, this is my fault! I feel so guilty. She helped me escape and now she will pay for it. He better not hurt her again! If he does, I'll hurt him twice as hard!

He was surprised at his imagined bravado, but his thoughts quickly returned to his own hopeless situation.

Twenty-Seven

There was a loud knock and Rainee's bedroom door burst opened. Two officers rushed in holding her cell phone. "Wake up, Signora Allen. They are calling."

Rainee stood straight up, her head fuzzy from a deep sleep. She did not recall lying down and wondered when sleep had defeated her. Daylight flooded the room. She glanced at the clock, stunned to see it was late afternoon.

She grabbed the phone and moved quickly into the other room, where every man was on alert. Fabrizio nodded and she pushed the "accept" button.

"Hello. It's Rainee Allen." She was still shaking the fuzziness of sleep.

"Did you get our picture yet?" the man on the other end of the line asked.

"No. What picture? What do you mean?" She was suddenly terrified. "What have you done?"

"We sent a picture of the boy to the police. I am surprised it is not spread all over Italy by now— and even to his father in California— and to you— his mama."

Rainee gasped and looked toward Fabrizio

"Si, we know why this rich boy is important to you. You gave him up, and now he gave you up. Believe me, Signora, when I say I had to beat it out of him. Oh, you should be a proud mama. It was not easy to get that information. You will see what I mean."

Rainee covered her mouth with her hands, afraid she might scream.

"And when you do see the picture, you will know that we mean business. We are sick of your games. Your delays. You cannot do this any longer. We will not stand for it. When you see his pretty face, just know that there will be much more of that– and worse!"

Rainee was shaking so hard, she could barely hold the phone. Her eyes filled with tears.

"Here are your instructions," Mickey Mouse said. "You are to bring the money tomorrow morning at exactly 11:00 a.m., and not one minute later. Time has run out. Go to the city of Montecchio Maggiore. It is about thirty-four kilometers from Verona. There are two castles there and a festival going on. Be on time. At the Castello della Villa, you will go to the second floor. You will see a *bagno* for signoras."

"What's a bagno?" she asked, trying to stall to lengthen the call.

"*Come si dice?*" His voice, though muffled, sounded annoyed as he searched for the right word. "Um... restroom? Si, restroom. You will put the money in *uno zaino...* oh, *Fanculo... como si dice?*" Again he muffled the phone. "Backpack. Si, backpack. You understand?"

"Yes."

"Put the backpack into the stall marked '*non funziona*'."

Rainee interrupted. "Does that mean 'out of order'?"

"Si. Then you must leave. We will go in when we see you leave the castle. Then—"

"But what about Joshua? Please don't hurt him anymore!"

"*Fanculo*! Do not interrupt me! I will do what I want until I have the money!" He exhaled a long breath. "You will be watched the entire time. There will be a gun pointed at the boy's head and a rifle at yours. You must come alone. If you do not do as I tell you, we will not hesitate to shoot him and you. I am not fooling around with this merda anymore. Do you understand me, Signora?"

"May I please ask a question now?"

"Si."

"I asked about Joshua. What about him? How do I know you won't kill him after you get the money?"

"We will let him go after we get the money. You go to the food area. He will be told where you are at the festival. He will go to you. You just have to look for Romeo." Then he laughed loudly. "*Buona fortuna.*" He laughed at his sarcasm.

Rainee was puzzled at his reference. "What? Why? What do you—"

There was a click and then silence.

She looked around at the police in the room. Her hands were shaking and she was as scared as she had ever been. "If they hurt him, I swear, I'll—" She could not finish the sentence.

Fabrizio looked concerned for her, then gave her some good news. The trace was successful.

Twenty-Eight

Jana returned home from school, kissed her grandmother, then went into her room for a needed nap.

Paloma unpacked Jana's backpack. She removed Jana's *Finding Nemo* lunchbox and opened it to find a half-eaten tuna salad sandwich, an untouched bag of apple slices, an empty bag of potato chips, and a half-empty juice box.

Her grandchild's kindergarten class always sent homework. While digging around for it, she removed an unsealed, unaddressed envelope.

Paloma wheeled herself to the table to read it under the fan light.

This note is for Rainee Allen. Make sure she gets this message.

We know about your relationship to Joshua Greenberg. You see that we know about your family in London. Now you see how we can get to them. Do as you are instructed and make sure that we get the money from his father without any more problems! Do not be foolish. If you get in the way of us getting the money, something very bad may happen to your little girl. You would not want to lose two of your children, would you? You have been warned! Viva Brigate Rosse!

Eyes wide with terror, Paloma immediately wheeled over to make sure her granddaughter was still in her room napping. She exhaled a sigh of relief and checked the doors and windows to make certain they were locked. Then she called Martin.

Twenty-Nine

Joshua sat alone in his cellar room. His chest and hips hurt from having the big man tackle him to the ground and sit on him. He could not be sure, but he may have a broken nose. His entire body was black and blue from being used as a punching bag. His night was sleepless.

He listened as the front door of the house opened and some of the men engaged in conversation. They suddenly started laughing. He wondered what they could be laughing about but did not have to wait long for the answer.

The key turned in the lock and the door swung open.

A man named Edoardo came in and threw colorful clothes on the bed. "Hey, rich boy, put this on. It will be perfect for you!" He turned and left.

Joshua looked at the ornate costume and recognized the style. It was the dress of an Italian nobleman in the late 1500s, complete with a short cape, tights, a hat with a large, purple plume, and slipper-like shoes. He pushed it away and sat back on the bed.

Ten minutes later, he heard a key in the lock and Tomasso walked into the room. "I thought we told you to put this on! Do it. Now!" he yelled. "Now!"

Joshua realized he had no choice but to comply, so he pulled the clothes closer to him. He hesitated for a few seconds, but Tomasso showed no signs of leaving.

Finally he slipped his pants off and pulled on the tights.

The ruffled shirt and the coat looked funny, but they fit him well.

As he left the room, Tomasso said, "You look good in rich man's clothes, rich boy. Now, take them off before you get them dirty."

Late morning was quiet, especially after all the early morning commotion. To make it worse, the room was still very cold.

Joshua's mind wandered incessantly. One thought that would not leave him was his father's accident. It must have happened as his father raced to the airport to try to bring him back. Joshua's emotions were overwhelming.

He feared that his father would not survive, and he worried about Deborah. She must be an emotional mess, with both her men in peril.

And Rainee. How would she be taking all this? He knew she was smart and was trying her best to find him, but she would also be going through her own emotional experience.

He felt especially alone because he felt disconnected from his father who had always been the most important and supportive person in his life. With Joshua's maturity, he was truly a friend. And they were more than six thousand miles apart during the worst period in either one's life. The painful sadness grew stronger each time he thought about his dad lying in a hospital bed, worrying about his son.

Memories of his life with his father flooded his mind. He thought about how much he really loved his life with his dad.

Joshua's earliest memories centered around watching his father sit in an old comfortable easy chair reading books in their small apartment in San Francisco.

Ricky developed a passion for computer software. He spent many nights reading about programming, learning every software he could get his hands on.

After he earned his Master's degree from UCSF, Ricky started a fledgling software business. With a unique and extraordinarily efficient software platform that would eventually revolutionize every computer, the business grew. He named it after his son, Joshware Media. In under four years, it became a publicly traded company on the Nasdaq Exchange under the ticker JWRE. It was not long before Ricky became well known and respected in the world-wide computer community.

Joshua was very proud that he was the namesake of the company and of course, he was also proud of his father. But the virtual world held no interest for him. His heart simply was not in it.

As a magna cum laude high school graduate, Joshua showed a superior intellect and a deep concern for global issues. He read numerous books on conflict-affected areas and inequality, violence, and security. He studied constructive ways to help move toward world peace. There was no doubt what he would study in college. Joshua Greenberg was relocating to the world stage. A relocation that would take him to the dingy root cellar he now occupied.

Thirty

"Why can't we leave now? You have their farm location. You could storm the farm. We could be there in no time. They think we are on our way from Rome." Rainee crossed her arms in defiance and began to pace. "This makes no sense to me, Fabrizio. No sense."

"Yes, they think we are in Rome. So we have six hours to prepare for this. If we surprise them, there is no telling what might happen to Joshua. I sent two men to check out the farm. They radioed back that there were multiple cars there. There is no way of knowing how many people are involved and how many are armed. They are watching the house now. We will be informed of any movement."

"But—"

"It is better to meet them at the appointed time and place. We have a better chance of getting Joshua out alive." Piscitelli waved his arm indicating the police who were all sitting and watching them. "We are all in agreement."

"But Fabriz—"

"Rainee, we have to assume they have weapons. How many? What kind? We have no way of knowing. You must be patient. We have to do this their way."

"Okay, this Romeo and Juliet Festival we will be going to... we will need costumes to blend in, too. Right?"

He turned to the men. "The signora has a good point. Gino, you and Paolo go into town and get costumes. And for God's sake, take off your suit jackets and look like tourists."

Fabrizio patted Rainee's shoulder. "But you will not need a costume. They are expecting you. Now, we must pass some time."

She went to the restroom. Her cell phone rang and it startled her. She quickly finished drying her hands and looked at the screen. Her husband's name lit up the screen.

"Hello Honey."

The reaction on the other end of the phone stunned her. "Rainee, we have a serious problem! You have to stop this now and let the officials handle Joshua!" His voice was shaky.

"What are you talking about, Martin? What's the matter?"

"Jana just brought home a note in her backpack. It was from one of those Red Brigade members threatening her safety if you interfere in any way with their receiving the money!"

"What? No!" She suddenly felt faint and needed to sit. She sat down hard on the toilet seat. "How? Oh my God, Martin! What should we do?"

"The first thing we're going to do is temporarily move Jana and my mum away from here. I'm sure Robert would let them stay with him for a while. He's a good mate. He has that big house with lots of room."

"Oh, Martin. I feel so awful putting you all in danger." She began to cry. "Sending them to Eastbourne is a good idea. Can you go today? My God, this is intolerable! How could they find us?" Rainee's revulsion for the group turned into pure hatred, accompanied by her own guilt.

Martin said, "I'm home now. I'll see to it that they are both ready to leave as soon as possible. They'll be fine as soon as we're at the cottage."

He took a deep breath. "Blasted! It's you I'm worried about! Rainee, these wankers are extremely desperate. They threatened the safety of a little girl, for God's sake! I don't think they would hesitate to harm you. I can't bear to have you in this position. I'm asking you— No, I'm begging you— No, I'm *ordering* you to let the police handle this. Please, come home."

Rainee responded with surprise at his demands. "Ordering? My God, Martin, Joshua is my son! No different than Jana. I gave birth to both of them and I have to protect both of them. As long as Jana, Paloma and you are safe, I will do what I must. We are so close to getting Joshua back. I can't stop now. I'm a part of the exchange process and it's happening today."

"Let the goddam police do their jobs, Rainee."

He had never raised his voice to her.

"Martin, you're not here. You don't know everything that is going on. And what right do you have to order me to do anything?"

"Rainee, be reasonable. If you won't consider your own safety, please think of your family's. I can't believe that you would allow your daughter to be put in a seriously dangerous position. These guys play for keeps! I've read up on them. You do not want to fool around with these killers. And make no mistake, they *are* killers. Please, Rain."

Rainee hesitated before she responded. "I understand, Martin. Don't you think this is killing me? I don't know what's right or wrong. On the one hand, my family is put in a position where they could be in danger. But they'll be moved to a safe place. On the other, my son is in *real* danger as we speak! If his father was here to help find him, that might be a different story, but he isn't! I am his only hope!"

"Listen to yourself, Rain!" Martin yelled back. "It's as if you think you're Superwoman and only you can save the day. It's just not reality. There are police involved. They are experts at this. They know what to do. Trust them and let them do their job. Please!"

"Look, I'm working with these guys. They're trying. They really are, but they just don't have a... a sense of urgency. They're not personally affected by this. Joshua is just a case number!" Her voice raised in pitch and volume. "I can't stand this, Martin! I need you to understand. I can't just walk away from my son and leave his safety, his very life in the hands of strangers who are just doing their daily job! Besides, I'm speaking with Joshua and he can hear my voice. That has to give him some kind of comfort. He knows that someone who cares is looking out for him. I cannot let him be alone, Martin! I won't!"

"I am begging you."

"And I am telling you that I need to see this through. Do I have to say it again? Joshua is my son, damn it! And I am surrounded by police carrying guns. I feel very protected and safe. Hearing that those animals were able to even get close to my daughter scares the hell out of me, but I know you're there to protect her. And I'm counting on you to do that."

There was a long pause. "I know, Rainee." Martin's voice softened. "I'm just so frightened that something might happen to you. You need to be extraordinarily careful, do you hear me? I can't lose you. Jana can't lose you. We need you, my love."

"I know. And I need you."

There was a moment of silence. "You know, you're like a bulldog. Once you've made your mind up, there is little I can do to change it. Don't worry, I'll take care of our little girl. You can't know how much I love you. Stay safe."

"I will, darling. I promise. Call me as soon as you are all safe at Robert's. I love you."

She wet her face again at the sink, dried it, then rushed quickly to Fabrizio, who was staring at a computer screen.

He looked up, the quickly made the screen go dark. "How can I help you, Rainee?"

"You say you can protect me? Well, what about my family? My little girl has been threatened by those animals! They sent a note home in her backpack! In her *backpack*! How could they have found her? I just don't understand!"

Fabrizio frowned. "Slow down. Try to calm yourself and tell me what happened."

"Calm myself? First my son, and now my daughter, my husband, and my mother-in-law are all in danger. And I put them in it. Me! Martin is furious with me. How can I possibly calm myself? Fabrizio, tell me. Tell me, please."

"I do understand your fear, Rainee. I will notify the London police. They will place some men to watch your home."

"That won't be necessary. Martin is going to move them to a friend's place outside the city."

"Well, that is good thinking, but probably unnecessary. You can trust me when I say, the Brigate Rosse are only trying to scare you. They will not do anything to your family."

"How can you know this? How can you be so sure? And if that's true, why notify the London police to watch my family at all?"

He sat her down. "Please, Rainee, put your trust in me. I have been doing this for a long time. We are trained to deal with terrorist organizations. They wanted to scare you, and they achieved that, did they not?"

"You bet your goddamn ass, they did."

"They just want the money. They will be getting it soon. Today. As I said before, they will not do anything to ruin those chances. It is all about the money. Let me tell you a little about them... the story behind this group." He took a sip of his espresso.

In a calming voice, Fabrizio began what sounded to Rainee like a lecture he must have repeated many times. "The original Brigate Rosse was started in 1967 by a leftist study group at a University. That's right. A study group. They dedicated themselves to the study of Che Guevara, Karl Marx, and Mao Tse Tung, among others. Their followers grew and soon there were hundreds around the world. They started as intellectuals and grew to be rebellious. I am not saying this to scare you."

Rainee nodded, "Yes, I read about them on the internet, which is why I am scared."

"Please allow me to continue. With organized and careful police work, the Brigate's leaders and members were arrested and imprisoned. By the 1980s, the organization was all but destroyed. This group is claiming to be them, but they are not. They are using the name to instill fear. They are just thugs looking for a big payout."

"Off."

"Scusami?"

"Payoff. That is the word you mean."

Fabrizio smiled. "Grazie... payoff. They are not in this for the true reasons the original Brigate Rosse were. These people have already tipped their hand, as you Americans say. They are sloppy. They think they are tougher than they are. But they are not."

Rainee shook her head. "But all it takes is just one of them, one fanatic, to harm my son or my daughter."

"Which is why we are being careful and methodical in our approach."

"But those pictures of Joshua... I can't seem to get them out of my head. He's hurt, Fabrizio. He is badly hurt."

"I understand, Rainee, and I am now sorry you saw them. I should not have allowed that. Joshua is young and strong. He will recover. The black and blue will go away with time. He will heal. And because they are making the exchange at the festival, he must be able to walk. The pictures make it seem worse than it really is. All I can ask of you now is to be patient and wait."

The waiting was the hardest part.

Rainee was exhausted and the worry was beginning to take its toll. Her patience was stretched to the limit. She had snapped at the police and even her movements were brusque. None of the men in the hotel room were rude to her. They seemed to understand the reasons for her frustrations and were tolerant and considerate.

What they did not understand was that Rainee felt they were being patronizing and in her mind, it felt as if they were trivializing the situation. If there was one thing Rainee hated, it was not being taken seriously.

As the men went about their job, she began to feel more and more invisible. The feelings of being ignored and insignificant riled her.

Fabrizio brought Rainee a cup of coffee and a sandwich. "May I sit?"

She had been sitting at a table staring at her cell phone. She looked up at him, with a slightly dazed look. "Certainly, Fabrizio. Please."

He placed the coffee and plate of food in front of her. "Rainee, I am concerned about you."

She expressed a quizzical look.

"I know this is taking quite a toll on you," he said, "but the money was wired, and we have it stacked in one hundred-dollar bills in the backpack. I hope it will not be too heavy for you. Maybe about ten or eleven kilograms on your back. Your daughter, she weighs more, si?"

Rainee nodded.

"Everything is going as planned. We are ready. You are ready."

Rainee gave him a look of incredulity.

"This is never an easy situation. For you. For everyone here. I just want to ease your fears. We have very competent men on this. They are also concerned about Joshua."

"But how could—"

"Believe me, Rainee. No one is taking this lightly. We are all aware of the seriousness of the situation."

"Situation? To you it's a situation. To me, it's a son I've never met. A life I missed out on. I know it was my choice, but— he needs me now. Joshua, Ricky, Deborah— they're all counting on me. How could—"

Rainee's voice cracked as she attempted to choke back her tears. This time it was useless. She broke down and sobbed.

Fabrizio moved his chair next to hers and put his hand on her shoulder. "It is okay, Rainee. We all understand. Go ahead, cry. You have been strong throughout this... this..."

"Mess. This is one helluva mess," she managed to eke out her words between sobs.

"Si, a mess."

"I am so scared. I don't like feeling weak, like this. I'm used to being in control, Fabrizio. Of situations, of my emotions." She took a deep breath and exhaled.

"Please, Rainee, eat some food."

"I don't—"

"Uh. You must do this for Joshua. You must be in control."

"Okay. You're right." Rainee managed a weak smile. She sat upright. With trembling hands, she sipped the coffee and took a bite of the pastry. She was scared for her family in London, but felt a little better knowing Martin had the situation under control.

Certainly they would all be safe at Robert's place.

Thirty-One

Still in pain and feeling scared, Daisy listened to the raucous group in the living room, drinking, telling off-color jokes and smoking cigarettes. *God, I hate them all.*

She lay in her bed thinking about how she would successfully escape this madness. Tomasso had someone nail the window shut, but she thought the small window in the WC did not look too secure. She might be able to remove a few nails and slip through.

She heard a key engage the lock on her door. Tomasso entered and sat down on the bed. He spoke quietly. He reached to gently stroke her face. "I am sorry I had to hit you, *la mia bellezza*, but you can understand. You left me. You left *us*. And you obviously tried to help our prisoner escape. That was not nice. You should not have done that. You see that now?"

Daisy remained motionless so as not to upset him. He kept caressing her while he spoke to her softly. She felt nauseated and scared. But she said and did nothing.

"Do you not see, *amore mio*, we have a good thing? In a few hours, we will be rich! Imagine. We will have enough money to go away on a wonderful *vacanza*. We can swim and sun on the beach during the day and make love all night long." He leaned forward and whispered in her ear, "Imagine how wonderful it is going to be."

Then he kissed her on the cheek.

She winced when he touched the spot where his fist had landed a powerful blow.

He expanded the area of his attention to include her forehead, her chin and ultimately her mouth.

Daisy did not kiss him back, but she also did not resist his advance. She did not know how to respond but figured she had better go along or risk upsetting him again.

It was not long before Tomasso's hands extended their caresses to include most of her body. His fervor and breathing increased rapidly. Without consent or a response from her, he quickly removed her clothes and got on top of her. He spread her legs and forcefully entered her.

When Tomasso was finished, he moved off her, zipped his pants and walked to the door. He looked back at her and winked. With a sneer on his lips, he waved, "*Ciao, bella.*"

The experience was humiliating and sickening. She simply endured the pain and let her mind wander to how she would leave this intolerable situation. She felt something for Joshua and wanted to help him. But she had to protect herself. She vowed that she would be out of there the first moment she had the opportunity.

She waited in her bed for a half-hour, then left her room.

Giorgio was guarding her door. "Where are you going, puttana?"

Daisy sneered at him. "The WC. Is that all right with you, fat man?"

He shrugged and closed his eyes for a quick nap.

Daisy used a tweezer to work on the small, nailed-shut window in the WC. She was confident she could squeeze through.

Less than five minutes later, she was running quickly and quietly through the field behind the house again. Fortunately, everyone assumed she was still in her room after Tomasso left it with a smile on his face. It was still daylight and she was free!

There were loud noises coming from upstairs. Lots of yelling and the thunderous sound of people running. Then someone stomped down the cellar steps.

The lock turned, the door flew open, and Tomasso stormed in.

Joshua stood, wondering what was wrong.

Tomasso threw a fast, hard punch and caught him in the gut. He saw stars and keeled forward.

A second punch connected with his already bruised cheek. Joshua flew back onto the bed, grimacing from the pain. He put up his hands to block any further facial assault.

Tomasso jumped onto him and grabbed his shirt and started shaking him as he ranted. "Where is she?" he screamed. "Where is that bitch? I know you know. You two seem to have some special relationship. Where did she say she was going?"

Joshua found himself unable to speak. He was in a state of shock. He realized Tomasso must be talking about Daisy. *Did she run again? When did she leave?* He didn't blame her for leaving, considering that she had been assaulted by Mickey Mouse's relentless verbal and physical attacks.

"I... I don't know," Joshua whimpered. He was weak and shaken, barely able to answer. "How could I? I've been stuck in this little box. I haven't seen her."

"Well, she better run fast and far, because when I catch up with her, she is a dead woman. Do you hear me? I will kill her! You better hope we do not find her! Or she will end up in a box, two meters down."

Joshua was frozen with fear.

Tomasso grabbed him and roughly pulled him up, then punched him in the gut again. He threw him against the bed and left the room.

Joshua keeled over in pain and vomited. He was scared for both himself and Daisy. There was no telling what Tomasso would do.

He lay moaning on the bed for hours. After a while, he heard more activity going on upstairs. There was muffled conversation. Something was definitely happening.

Then there was the distant sound of a knock on the front door. Someone of importance just arrived. Yes, he could feel it. A moment later, cheering started. It seemed like their guest had brought some good news. Everyone in the house sounded happy.

Twenty minutes passed. The noises blended into a cacophony of sound that Joshua interpreted as happiness and excitement. A few people tramped down the cellar steps. Then the lock in his door clicked.

A man dressed like a Renaissance executioner entered. He wore a mask and a black-hooded cloak, shrouding his face. Tomasso followed him in. One man stood guard outside the room.

"You see? He has a comfortable bed, a clean room and even a beautiful toilet!" said the leader. "He is like a guest in a five-star hotel! You wanted to see for yourself, and now you have seen. Now let us go back upstairs where we can have a nice drink, eh?"

The masked man nodded in agreement.

Before he left, Tomasso turned to Joshua. "You will be happy to know that the money has come through."

"You mean my Dad's okay?"

"I do not know. And I do not give a damn." He sneered. "Lorenzo– I mean Pluto– make sure he cleans up his face and dresses in the costume. Then bring him upstairs so we can all see. And make it quick, eh?" Tomasso turned and left the room. The door shut, and the footsteps of the men resounded as they climbed the stairs.

Joshua asked, "Who was that? I understand the hood and all, but why the mystery?"

Lorenzo said nothing.

When he was dressed, Joshua followed Lorenzo up the stairs where they joined the group in the main room. Even Tomasso seemed to be in a good mood. They all had a variety of alcoholic drinks in their hands, including the masked man.

"Here. Take a beer, Romeo!" Tomasso said. "The time has come for you to make us rich! All of us, except that stupid bitch who is going to miss out on this! Oh well, her loss is more for us! *Si, amici*?" Everyone raised their bottles and cheered.

Tomasso opened a bottle of Peroni and handed it to Joshua.

Joshua hesitatingly took it.

He drank in silence while the rest slapped each other's backs and spoke in elevated tones. All except the hooded man. He did not speak at all. At first, this puzzled Joshua, but consumed with his own thoughts of safety, he stopped thinking about it.

Joshua thought the beer he was drinking tasted especially good. He could have used another one but did not want to ask. No one offered, so he placed his empty bottle on a small table and stood silently, waiting to see what was going to happen. He did not have to wait long.

The sound of a car rolling over the pebbled drive in the front of the house was their cue. They all started gathering up their personal effects and their costumes. Each walked to their rooms, the WC and even the kitchen and started changing into their colorful outfits. Naturally, laughter started the moment the first of the group walked into the room dressed in their Renaissance costumes.

Lorenzo wore a fifteenth century blue and yellow doublet draped over a white frilly blouse which he tucked into yellow tights. His bulging belly draped over his tights. A short, multicolored cape draped his shoulders and old cuffed boots completed his look. It may not have been comical back in the 1500s, but no one in the room could tame their laughter. Even Joshua grinned.

They finished their fashion show punctuated with spasms of laughter and disparaging remarks delivered in jest, had one more beer and readied themselves to go to the exchange.

The hooded man whispered something to Tomasso, then nodded to the others and walked out the front door.

Tomasso followed, then turned to the group and said, "*Andiamo ragazzi*. Bring the kid. Let us go get rich!"

Thirty-Two

The trip from Verona to Montecchio Maggiore on the E70 would only take about forty minutes in Fabrizio's unmarked Gallardo. Rainee sat in the back seat behind dark-tinted windows.

According to plan, three other nondescript police vans arrived two hours before the rendezvous time and positioned themselves for optimum surveillance.

From the distance, Rainee could see two castles atop a hill with buildings dotting the hillside.

Fabrizio pointed. "See those two castles? The one on the right is Castello Bellaguardia, also known as Juliet's castle. The one on the left is Castello della Villa, Romeo's castle. That is the castle where you will leave the ransom."

"Really? They're astonishing." Rainee was enthralled.

"Si. They both were built around 975 A.D. and are said to be the inspiration for the legend of Romeo and Juliet."

Rainee said, "I had no idea that there was an actual legend and not just the play."

Fabrizio laughed. "Si. There are many variations on the story told many times since the fourteen-hundreds. The theme of star-crossed lovers was borrowed from poets as far back as ancient Greece. So Romeo and Juliet's tale was told at least a century before Shakespeare even wrote it."

"You seem to know a lot about the story."

"I grew up in this area. Just outside of Verona. You cannot live here and not know about Shakespeare."

They passed a billboard announcing *La Faida*, the Romeo and Juliet Festival. The sign showed a picture of Juliet leaning on her balcony, with Romeo looking up from below.

"Fabrizio, if everyone is dressed in costumes— and I assume all the staff working there will be in costume too— how will the police know the bad guys from the good guys?"

"We can only hope they're not smart enough to wear masks. Not everyone does. And, you don't often see men walking about without a wife and a family at these things. So, individual men may tip their fingers."

"Hand. Tip their hand." She immediately regretted correcting him again. "I'm so sorry," she sighed.

"It is okay, Rainee. It is good for me to learn how to say words correctly. Anyway, we also look for nervous, suspicious behaviors, like looking over their shoulders frequently. And we will watch for people who are paying too much attention to the restroom where the drop will happen. Do not forget that my men have been in position now for a couple of hours. They are on the roof with binoculars, they are in booths acting like vendors."

Rainee began to feel apprehensive, not knowing what would lay ahead.

Fabrizio pulled into the jam-packed festival parking lot. Volunteers were directing cars into spaces. The detective exited his car and donned his mask. He looked at his watch, "Good. We are on time."

Fabrizio handed Rainee the backpack with the money. She lifted it onto her back with a little grunt.

"Heavy?"

"I can manage it. My daughter weighs more than this. I was just a little surprised, that's all." The pack was over twenty-five pounds, but it was a tall one made for long hikes and camping, so its size was a bit overwhelming.

He instructed Rainee to walk in front of him. "You will not see me, but I will not let you out of my sight. Just remember what we told you. No heroics, even if you see any of them. Just leave the pack in the designated place, walk away and do not look back. Go to our meeting point and Federico will meet you there just as we planned it, *capisci*?"

Rainee nodded.

He put his hand on her shoulder. "You can do this. You, Signora Allen, are one strong and brave lady."

Rainee wished at that moment she had the same confidence in herself that he had in her.

She paid for her ticket, entered the grounds, and took in the surroundings. The ambiance was enchanting. There were knights, princesses, and noblemen parading around in full costume. There were food stands and historical festivities, and entertainers like jugglers, musicians, and court jesters.

A metal sign pointed the way to Romeo's Castello. Rainee followed the winding path to deliver the money. She was nervous because she knew there were eyes on her, both good and bad.

Both castles sat atop a hill, so it was an uphill path and the weight of the backpack caused her to lose her balance more than once. Beads of perspiration formed on her neck, but adrenaline kept her moving forward.

"Damn it!" The path forked, and she was unsure which way to go.

She witnessed two mischievous children redirecting the arrows which pointed the way to the castle. "Hey!" she yelled. The children giggled and ran off. *Little brats! Where are their parents?* she wondered with exasperation.

Rainee hoped that all paths would eventually merge and lead to Romeo's Castle. *Just take your best shot, Rainee.*

Gathering her strength, she took the left path, but soon she realized that no other visitors had taken that path. She was alone. Forging on, the path became thinner and the brush became denser.

"Shit. Shit. Shit. I should've gone right. Now I have to retrace my steps, and I'm losing time."

She could see the tower of the castle looming ahead, but she was off the path. She would have to push her way through the brush. But it was too thick and she decided that it would be better to turn back.

The realization hit her that there was a possibility no eyes were on her now. *Fabrizio must be wondering where I am.* There was freedom to move about, but she was not in costume and could not take that chance. Nor could she take the chance of falling behind the scheduled drop off and perhaps putting Joshua in jeopardy. However, she took a few moments to catch her breath.

Rainee turned around and found going downhill with the backpack a real challenge.

Two young teenage boys, playing hide and seek from their parents, cut through in front of her. They took a path on her left. She quickly yelled out, "*Scusami.*" The boys turned around. Rainee asked, "Do you speak English?"

"Yeah. We're from Canada," the taller boy said.

"Oh good. Does the path you're on lead directly to Romeo's castle? I got a little lost back there."

"Yeah. Follow us."

A short distance later she emerged onto the green that surrounded the castle. She waved to the boys. "Thanks, guys."

From where she emerged, she could plainly see the correct path she would have taken had she not got turned around. Visitors in abundance, came ambling through a great white arch which declared in Shakespearean font "Welcome" in several different languages.

Rainee expected to see Fabrizio searching for her. She scanned the green that led to the cobblestoned entrance of the castle. In the distance, she saw him.

He was not looking around for her. He was standing with a gentleman in a long black cloak, holding his mask. They were standing unusually close to each other, their foreheads nearly touching. Fabrizio and the man were having a very animated discussion. *Or is it an argument?* Both men's hands weaved through the air punctuating their conversation, not unusual for Italians, but there was finger pointing, as well.

A few moments later, Fabrizio left in a hurried walk.

Rainee slowly approached the hooded man. She had recognized him from his pictures. It was Joshua's mentor.

"Why Professor Esposito! What a surprise."

Thirty-Three

The group gathered what they needed, and it did not escape Joshua's notice that most of them pocketed handguns. They filed out of the front door to the waiting vans.

Tomasso and another man led Joshua out of the back door to a mahogany brown van parked behind a shed.

The drive was made in silence. When the van drove onto the unpaved parking area, Joshua knew they had arrived. Only then did he start to worry. *What if something goes wrong with the exchange? Dad send the money? What if there is no money? Will they kill me?* He could hear his own heart beating loudly in his ears.

The others checked their weapons and placed them in whatever places they could find in their costumes.

The vans parked and they all got out.

"Not so fast, Romeo," said Lorenzo. "Put out your hands. I am going to tie them together. You and I wait here until we are told to go." The man used a rough piece of twine to tie Joshua's hands together. It was too tight, but he didn't complain.

He settled back into his seat. The others walked toward the castle.

Thirty-Four

Stunned for a few seconds, the professor finally said, “I'm sorry, I don't believe we've met.”

“Rainee Allen. It's good to meet you, sir.” Rainee stuck out her hand. “Of course, it would be better under different circumstances.”

Having regained his composure, the professor kissed her hand. “Ah yes, Joshua's biological mother. Truly an honor. Different circumstances indeed. You have a remarkable son. One of my brighter students. I'm so very sorry this has happened. I know he was looking forward to meeting you in Venice.”

She nodded. “He spoke highly of you.”

“Um, Rainee, uh... the detective and I have been in touch regarding Joshua's kidnapping since I was interviewed back in Rome.

I have been consumed with worry, as you can imagine. The last time we spoke, Detective Piscitelli said he was headed to the Romeo and Juliet Festival. Naturally, I came immediately. I want to help in any way I can.”

“Of course.” Rainee smiled, but her innate curiosity was peaked. *Strange that Fabrizio didn't mention this to me.*

Rainee thought his voice of concern sounded disingenuous but was worried about the time. "I must get to the drop point. I hope to speak with you soon professor."

"And I, you. Another time, Ms. Allen."

Gravity's tug on her backpack was nothing compared to the nagging tug in her brain. *There is more going on than he let on. No time to think about it though. The sooner I get this money delivered, the sooner I see Joshua. And the sooner he is safe.*

As she walked away, she felt the familiar tingle of her phone vibrating in her pants pocket. She pulled out the two cell phones thinking it could have been the kidnappers. It was Martin. She stuck the phones back in her jacket pocket.

Looking for someone to ask directions, she stopped a docent to inquire where the stairs were for the restroom. The docent directed her to the first-floor ladies room, where all the tourists were. She realized her error and headed in that direction so as not to attract attention by the staff. She would have to locate it herself.

Fortunately for Rainee, all the signs were in English, French, and Italian. She moved with purpose toward the main staircase, where people were ascending and descending.

"*Scusami, Signora, posso essere di aiuto?*" The young docent's smile lit up his face like the colorful regalia he wore. He was young and beautiful and could easily be Shakespeare's Romeo.

Rainee did not answer immediately, so he asked again in English. "Is there some way I can help you?"

"Oh, perhaps you could direct me to the second-floor restroom. I need to change into my costume."

"Sure. Just follow me."

Rainee took no notice of the masked woman in the flowing, crimson red costume following closely behind her.

Thirty-Five

Joshua thought he might be able to find out some information from Lorenzo, so he started talking to him. First he asked questions about the fair.

At first Lorenzo didn't answer him, but after a while he did out of sheer boredom.

After a few minutes of general discussion about the event, Joshua asked, "If the money is there and your guys pick it up, will you let me go?"

Lorenzo said nothing at first, then put his hand on his weapon. "*Silenzio!*"

Then Joshua saw something out the front window of the van that got his attention.

Flashing colored lights reflected off the windshield. *It's the police! Should I start screaming?*

Before he thought it through, he rolled onto the floor and started to kick the side of the van with his feet, yelling, "Help!" as loud as he could.

Lorenzo jumped over the back of the seat and pointed the gun directly at his face.

Joshua stopped.

Lorenzo pistol-whipped Joshua in the face, knocking him out. He jumped back into the front seat and rolled down the window in time to hear the officer's inquiry.

"*Cosa sta succedendo lì*? What is going on in there? Did I hear someone yelling?"

"Oh. Uh... yes sir... yes sir. My... uh... nephew is in the back and was insisting we go into the festival, but I told him that we were waiting for his madre to arrive. He was just mad. That is all."

"Where is he now? Have him step out of the van," demanded the officer.

"Okay. Sure," said Lorenzo, who pocketed the gun as he stepped out the passenger door.

The two stood in front of the side doors. Lorenzo took a handkerchief from his pocket and wiped the sweat from his brow. He turned the handle, and said, "Giovanni, come talk to the nice officer. He just wants to talk to you."

While the officer looked for a young boy to emerge, Lorenzo took his weapon out of his pocket. He slammed the officer's head with the pistol.

The officer dropped to the ground.

Lorenzo picked him up and slid him into the van.

He knew the mess he had on his hands. Not only would he have to contend with Joshua when he came to, but he also had an unconscious officer of the law in the back of the van— and he was parked next to a police car with its lights flashing! Whatever he was going to do, he would have to do immediately.

He moved quickly to the driver's side door of the van, opened it and dropped his pistol on the seat. Then he hopped in and turned the key. He had to get away.

As he put the van in reverse, someone pounded on the passenger window. "Where is the poliziotto who was here? Open the door!"

He was surprised to see another officer. And the man was drawing his gun.

Lorenzo had no choice but to do the same. He grabbed his weapon and fired wildly.

Glass burst outward and the van filled with the ear-shattering explosion. The officer outside of the van was no longer in sight.

Lorenzo pulled the shift lever down to reverse and jammed the accelerator. The van lurched backwards and slammed into a car parked behind it in the next row. Lorenzo shifted into drive, turned the wheel and put his foot down hard on the accelerator. The wheels spun on the grass, then gained purchase and the car lunged forward just in time for Lorenzo to see the body of the officer lying on the ground and to hear someone yell, "*Che cazzo?*"

The van raced away from the scene as Lorenzo glanced into the side mirror.

A group of onlookers were staring after him with their mouths open. Then they scattered like roaches suddenly exposed to light. Another officer with his gun drawn was coming up behind him.

The van sped down the grassy lane between rows of parked cars. In the rear view mirror, the previously knocked-out officer in the rear of the van rose to his knees and felt around for his handgun.

Lorenzo knew he had very little time. He made a fast ninety-degree turn and the man fell over and tumbled. Then the van stopped suddenly and he managed to gain his balance.

But it was too late. Lorenzo twisted around and pointed his gun directly at the man's head. He pulled the trigger, and another ear-shattering gun blast filled the van. Lorenzo could then hear nothing, including the sound of Joshua screaming at him.

Joshua was shaken to the core. A man was killed right next to him. He was trembling, while holding his tied hands over one ear, then the other. He had never experienced any sound as loud as a confined gunshot.

Lorenzo shoved the front door open, then jumped out of the van. He opened the sliding door and grabbed Joshua by his arm. He pulled Joshua out violently over the body of the dead man and looked at the castle. Lorenzo took off on a run, pulling Joshua behind him. They headed towards the castle grounds. The parking lot would soon be swarming with more police.

Joshua was visibly shaken, but relieved that he had not been shot. It was not easy, running with his hands tied together. He fell down almost immediately, but Lorenzo yelled at him to get up.

Joshua turned to look down the lane toward where the first officer had been shot. A crowd was gathering quickly. Many were pointing toward them and yelling to other officers.

Thirty-Six

Rainee was startled by a loud noise. She thought she heard a gunshot but wasn't sure. *Could it have been a car backfiring?* She listened intently and saw she was not alone. Everyone around her seemed to be aware that there was a loud, out-of-place crack, but no one could be certain. When she heard the second shot, she knew and was terrified.

There was no doubt in her mind that it was the sound of a gun firing. Rainee had heard that same sound on an overcast London day when she had taken the elderly Jana for a walk. She never saw the face of the thug who had shot at her, but the crack of the bullet was not something she ever got out of her head.

She cried out, "Joshua! Oh my God, Joshua!" In a panic, she ran out of Romeo's castle toward where she thought the crack came from— the festival's entrance. Rainee disregarded the money on her back. If Joshua had been shot, there would be no exchange. If he was not shot, she would hand over the money to whomever had the gun. She couldn't just stand there and do nothing. *I need to find Joshua!*

Five million Euros is not light, but the weight of the backpack didn't slow her down. Adrenaline was flowing in her veins, like a wild white-river ride.

The scene following the second gunshot was pure chaos. People started running toward the forested areas. Some ran to the castle, and some hid behind the vendor tents. It was pandemonium.

Rainee had always managed to keep level-headed and clear-thinking. Her panic over Joshua was conjoined with strategizing her next move. She knew that if there were still eyes on her with all of this confusion, she had better keep on the move. She had to help Joshua, but perhaps she was better off finding Fabrizio first.

Using the crowd as cover, she moved behind a large statue of a Renaissance man. She peeked around it trying to find him through the mass of tourists. *He's a cop. He must have headed toward the shots. It did sound like it came from the parking area. I'm sure of it. I have to get there.*

Rainee moved quickly, still using the panicked crowd as cover. The woman in red followed only steps behind her.

Thirty-Seven

"Merda!" said Tomasso. "Who was that? Who shot the gun?" He picked up his pace and headed toward the drop point. The money took precedence, not who shot whom.

Lorenzo was struggling, trying to pull Joshua over the uneven grassy terrain. He fell to one knee more than once, tearing his black tights and dragging Joshua down with him each time. Occasional glances over his shoulder at the group of people looking in their direction encouraged him to move as fast as possible. Several times he lost his grip on the uncooperative Joshua, but each time he managed to grab hold of his arm more firmly. They were getting closer to his goal.

He jammed the gun into Joshua's back. "Keep moving!"

Lorenzo was terrified and losing it. *I should not have shot those officers. Merda! But what was I supposed to do? I cannot handle this alone. Tomasso will know what to do.*

He needed to get lost in the crowd, then reach the castle and find Tomasso fast. The officers would catch up with him very soon.

While Lorenzo was preoccupied with worry, Joshua was able to loosen the rope that bound his hands. His hands were free. And

Lorenzo kept looking back to check on him and to see who was following.

In what seemed like slow motion, a scenario he could hardly believe, Joshua turned left, shoving the gun away from his back. Then his own balled fist cleaved the air and found Lorenzo's left temple. It dropped him like a stone, leaving him unconscious.

I can't believe it worked! I knocked him out!

He turned his head to see a man in uniform running toward him. He would normally be happy to see him, but Rainee was somewhere in that castle and he needed to find her fast. She was there with the money to rescue him and most likely in danger herself. He could not spend the time it would take to explain everything to the officer. After all, the man couldn't possibly know Joshua was not the one who shot the other officers.

He glanced at the castles on the hill. If he ran fast, it would take him less than two minutes to reach the entrance fence. He made a quick decision. The lone officer would have his hands full, especially since Lorenzo was regaining consciousness, with a gun beside him on the ground.

Joshua needed to go. He pivoted and took off.

Running at top speed, Joshua arrived at the entrance. He had no money on him so he walked along the perimeter fence until he found a spot where he would not be seen and quickly jumped over it. He landed hard and almost yelled out in pain from the bruises Tomasso had inflicted on him. But he had made it inside the fair grounds.

Where he stood, it was green and heavily wooded. Through patches of trees, he could see merchants and performers of the period everywhere. A sign pointed left toward the Juliet castle and right toward the Romeo castle. *Where to go?* It was a 50/50 choice.

He turned right toward the Romeo castle.

Thirty-Eight

Running on adrenaline, Rainee moved toward the food vendor area, convinced that she would find Joshua there. An unexpected composure came over her. It was the same calm she experienced when she protected Jana Lutken from skin-heads in a London park a few years ago. It was that same calm she experienced when her daughter, little Jana, walked impulsively into a busy street to chase down a balloon.

On that occasion, adrenaline coursed through her and her maternal instincts took over. Her mind clear, she maneuvered through the crowded traffic like a superhero and rescued her daughter from an oncoming truck. It was not until they were safely on the sidewalk that her adrenaline-ridden body began shaking, as she clutched little Jana in a tight embrace.

Rainee ignored these feelings as she headed full speed toward the area where she hoped she would find Joshua. She was no superhero. She was a mother.

An arm reached out and grabbed her shoulder, almost knocking her off her feet. “Professor!”

“Ms. Allen, follow me. I know a safe place.”

"No. No, I have to get to Joshua."

"Please, you must listen to me. Piscitelli told me everything. You have the money. That's all they want. Once you give it to them, they'll have no use for you or Joshua. They are very bad men. Follow me and let the police do their job. I can keep you safe."

Every cell in her body told her no. "I have to get to Joshua."

"Listen to me, Ms. Allen, I know you want to help. The police are closing in on them. They will protect Joshua. Follow me." He spoke with a new insistence, tugging on her arm.

Against her better judgement, she followed him. Moving through a denser part of the trees to avoid the path, she asked, "Professor, how do you know Detective Fabrizio?"

"Oh, well, um... he interviewed me back in Rome. Right after Joshua was kidnapped. I told him all I could."

"I see. How did you know we were in Verona?"

Moving branches out of their way, he said, "Piscitelli kept me informed. I called him nearly every day for information on Joshua."

He had side-stepped her question. Rainee could tell from his tone, he was becoming impatient, almost annoyed by her inquiries. *Odd that Fabrizio never told me about his calls.*

"Tell me, how did you recognize me?"

"Joshua showed me a picture of you. He keeps a picture on his cell phone. Really, Ms. Allen, let's just concentrate on getting the money— and you— to a safe place."

They heard the shrill sound of a nearby police whistle. The professor crouched.

Avoidance. Why would he need to avoid the police? Rainee stopped in her tracks. Her instincts were telling her that something was very wrong. She shook her head. "This isn't right. I must get to Joshua."

Professor Esposito pulled a gun out of his cape. He pointed it at Rainee. "I've had enough of this. Move. Move now."

Rainee's eyes widened and she did exactly what he demanded of her.

Thirty-Nine

Joshua heard the police whistle and looked behind him. Two officers ran past him so he started walking faster. He had no idea where to look for Rainee. He wondered if she was costumed or even if he would recognize her. He had an image of her in his mind, since he had seen many professional pictures of her on the internet and her book jackets, but she could look much different.

He even had one hanging on his bedroom wall, but it was of her when her first novel became a hit and she was younger. His dad and Deborah never discouraged it. In fact, they liked that he took some pride in his biological mother's success.

Rainee could be gray-haired now, no longer brunette. Her hair might be long, not short. She could be obese. He wished they had exchanged pictures before he left for Europe.

He maintained his quick pace as he tried to lose himself in the throngs of people. He was costumed, but he had no mask to hide his beaten face.

There, not thirty feet in front of him, was a busy vendor tent with the signage, *The Merchant of Venice*.

He wondered what he should do. He had no money with him, but he really needed a mask to get lost in the crowd. And this was a life or death situation. He ducked into the shop and casually meandered around the crowded, and makeshift store. He loitered near a table that displayed masks. He removed his cloak and placed it over the table.

He kept his eyes on the lone clerk, an elderly woman.

When she turned to answer a customer's question, Joshua grabbed a mask and walked out into the crowd. He ripped off the price tag and donned the mask, then glanced around to see whether anyone had noticed.

No one had.

Forty

Rainee moved branches out of her way as she walked, silently hoping they were slapping Esposito. Her calm was replaced by confusion. "Professor, why? Why are you doing this?"

"No questions. Just move. Bear to the left here."

"Please. Don't you care about Joshua?"

"I said no questions. Now keep going straight."

They came to the end of the clearing, and Juliet's castle came into view. This was not the designated drop-off.

People were slowly emerging from hiding, assuming that the police had everything under control.

Esposito put the gun under his black cape and pressed it against Rainee's back. He whispered, "Don't do anything stupid. Keep moving. Act normal."

They entered the garden, where people were looking up at the famous balcony, known as the place from Shakespeare's play where Romeo professed his dying love for Juliet.

Nobody noticed them.

"Keep moving." Esposito's voice was menacing.

They came to a door with a sign that read, *Under repair. Keep out.* It was unlocked. Esposito reached past Rainee to open it and they started down a dark hallway that had been chained off. He removed the chain.

"Where are we going?"

"Keep moving. Juliet's tomb room is a fitting place, I think."

"I don't understand. You could have taken the money in the forest. Why didn't you?"

"There were too many police running around."

"Take it now." She turned and offered him the backpack. "I don't want it. I just want my son."

"Not here," he said. "Keep going. The tomb room is walled with stone. Very quiet. Very insulated."

They descended a winding, uneven staircase.

Rainee balanced herself by touching the ancient walls.

Esposito stopped on a landing and said, "Wait."

He removed his cell phone and placed a call. Considering how far out in the countryside they were, and the thickness of the stone walls, Rainee was surprised to hear a dial tone. Then there was a recording. "Dammit! Tomasso! Tomasso, change of plans. Meet me at Juliet's tomb. I have the money. Do not hurt the boy. I hope you get this in time."

The sound of a loud thud surprised Rainee. She turned around to see a woman dressed in crimson. She held a bloodied rock in her hand.

The professor was on the ground, unconscious. Blood trickled from the back of his head.

"Who are you?"

The woman removed her mask. She had dark eyes and long black hair. She was beautiful and exotic-looking, resembling a young Sophia Loren. "My name is Giulietta. I am a friend of your son."

"Giulietta? He never mentioned you."

Giulietta lowered her head. "He did not meet me until he was taken. I was one of the group who captured him. He knows me as Daisy. But he was kind to me. I escaped these men— these cruel men— and I want to help you save Joshua. He is a good man and he was kind to me. They are fools." She spat on the floor with disgust.

Rainee looked down at the body sprawled on the stairs. "Is he dead?"

"*Non los so.* I mean, I do not know. And I do not care. He was the leader of the Brigate Rosse." She picked up his cell phone.

"I don't understand. How could that be? He was a respected university professor in the United States! He was well-known. Joshua looked up to him."

"He used Joshua because he knew his father was wealthy. This plan was in the making for years."

"I can't believe it."

Giulietta crouched and deftly rummaged through the pockets of the professor's slacks. She pulled out his wallet, then fished through it and retrieved a picture. "Here." She straightened and gave it to Rainee.

Rainee frowned. "Who is this?"

"It is the professor. Maybe thirty years ago. Notice the bandana and the flags. Look at the symbols. The Brigate Rosse. He waved it around, showing everyone one night at the farmhouse several months ago. The men were all drinking. It was a boast-fest."

Rainee nodded. "In America, we call it a pissing contest." She squinted, then pointed. "Who is this younger man in the corner? His face is familiar."

"Oh, that is his nephew. I hear he is polizia now."

Rainee shook her head in disbelief. It was Fabrizio.

Of course, that was why the young man in the picture had looked familiar to her. No wonder Fabrizio didn't want to send the picture she found on the web to Interpol. It was him. He had dismissed the idea. And he showed frustration when the money transfer was delayed. Those feelings of suspicion she had were for a good reason. She should have followed her instincts.

"Not only that but look at this younger boy's face. He, too, is that man's nephew. His name is Tomasso. He is the man who took your son. He is responsible for the resurgence of the Brigate Rosse, and he is very dangerous! He is the one who beat your son up. He will not hesitate to kill both of us if he sees us. He is here right now, looking for the money."

Rainee was wide-eyed. The puzzle was coming together, but there were still pieces missing.

Fabrizio had shown kindness and concern toward her. He always insisted she rest and eat. And he took an oath to become a detective.

Perhaps having a fugitive uncle was why he swore to protect the people of Italy.

But no, there were still too many pieces missing.

This play was quickly coming to a climax. Like in a fitting Shakespeare drama, the denouement would reveal the truth.

A sense of urgency overcame her. "My God! I have to get to Joshua!"

She stared at Giulietta. "Fabrizio is here! He may be working with the professor! He could even be part of the kidnapping! I can't be sure, but we must get to Joshua!"

"Not with that money on your back. First, we will hide the backpack. Otherwise they will kill you and Joshua— and me."

"But where? If Tomasso hears the message, he will head straight to the tomb."

"No, we must go to the kitchen. I worked here once. There were many large clay pots with heavy lids. It will fit in one of those. Let us hope they are still there."

"Lead on, Giulietta. I am in your hands."

The professor fought his way back to consciousness just in time to hear Giulietta's suggestion.

He watched as the women turned away.

Forty-One

Joshua looked in every direction but could not see Rainee. Of course, it didn't help that most people were wearing masks or elaborate wigs and makeup. *What if I can't find her? How will I be able to contact her?*

He froze. A man wearing the costume that Tomasso had put on in the van walked right past him.

That's him!

Tomasso would not recognize him because he was now wearing a mask and had rid himself of the rented cloak. Thankfully, he was walking away quickly.

It was unnerving being this close to his captor. Joshua seemed unable to move his legs. If he waited too long, Tomasso would be nowhere in sight.

He must be going to the castle, and Rainee will most likely be there. I'll follow him. I should be able to stay close without him detecting me. He turned around and started walking quickly toward Juliet's castle.

As he made his way along the crowded thoroughfare, Joshua kept an eye out for Rainee and thought how difficult the masks made it to spot anyone. *If I wasn't wearing my mask, she would probably recognize me, but that's too dangerous. Any one of those assholes who kidnapped me would recognize me.*

They must have heard the gun shots. But no one is running toward the parking lot, so maybe they don't know what happened. Most likely the gang doesn't know I'm free and on the castle grounds.

His vision was hampered by the mask's small eyeholes. He tripped on a cobblestone and went down painfully to one knee, ripping his tights. Blood began to ooze from the bad scrape. When he stood up, he had lost sight of the fast-moving Tomasso.

It was a warm day, and beads of sweat were forming on his brow as he negotiated the crowded walkways.

He had overheard Tomasso instructing Rainee about the money drop point. *It was a bathroom somewhere, but where? Is it even in this castle?* He wished he had paid more attention to that conversation.

As he approached the castle, he walked toward the first sign that read *Bagno Pubblico* and beneath it in English, *Public Restroom.*

The arrow indicated a small pathway to the left. He walked past the sign and there seemed to be no activity. He walked into the men's room, but nobody was in it.

More likely it would be in the women's room. It was a few steps behind him.

He watched and waited as several women walked in and out of the room. After several minutes of seeing no one emerge, he peeked in and saw that all the stalls were in working order.

It must be the wrong place. He went to look for other public restrooms.

When he emerged into a public square, he found himself in a tight crowd of people watching some swordplay, convincingly performed by hired actors.

What I wouldn't give to have a real sword in my hand right now.

A smaller crowd was listening to musicians playing instruments of the period.

He moved slowly, always keeping an eye out for anyone he might recognize. He made his way to the other side of the castle where he found another restroom. This time, there were several men inside. No one he recognized, though.

A quick check of the women's room told him these rooms were not where he needed to be. He kept searching inside the castle itself for another sign showing *Bagno Pubblico.*

A young family was descending the steps to the second level. The young English girl said, "Why was that loo closed, Mummy? I really have to go!"

Closed! There are more bathrooms upstairs! That sounds right. He bolted up the stairs two at a time to a sign that read in Italian and English, *Restrooms Closed for Repair. Use first floor facilities, please. We're Sorry for the Inconvenience.*

Since no one was around, he entered and looked around the room. He looked under each stall, found no one, then looked in the trash bin. Nothing. Dismayed, he walked back out into the hallway.

Some people milling around a sign that read, *Balcony Re-enactment.* It listed several performances throughout the day. He walked toward the group and realized the event had already begun. He saw the back of an actress leaning on the balcony, reciting her lines.

Joshua noticed a window to the right of the famous balcony. He walked over, hoping to get a good view of the small courtyard. He leaned out and scanned the crowd.

His gaze was drawn to a woman dressed in red. He was shocked to see Rainee walking beside her.

He leaned out and yelled her name.

People on the ground looked up, annoyed at the young man yelling next to the actress playing Juliet. She glanced over, too. He was suddenly the center of attention, but he didn't care. He had found Rainee and most likely would not have another chance. If he ran back through the castle, it would take too long to locate her again.

The time to act was now.

Forty-Two

Less than five minutes before, Giulietta had moved quickly through the castle and its winding hallways. Her pace caused Rainee to become breathless, trying to keep up with the twenty-something. They had deposited the backpack in a large kitchen urn, the height of which came up to Rainee's waist. They were now out of the castle and on their way to look for Joshua.

Rainee knew she was heading into possible peril with a dangerous, armed Brigate Rosse faction and possibly even Fabrizio. She was still shocked and conflicted with the news of Fabrizio's relationship to the professor. Was he a good man or was he bad? Could she trust him with Joshua's life, and with her own?

And Giulietta was a new character in this play. Rainee was following her blindly, but could she trust her? How could Rainee know for sure? They might be heading into a maelstrom of violence, but she had little choice. She had followed her instincts thus far and every cell in her body told her to keep going forward.

They exited the castle below Juliet's balcony, unaware that the re-enactment had begun. The crowd's eyes were turned upward toward the actress playing Juliet, who was resting on her palm, sighing Romeo's name.

Giulietta said, "This way."

They did not notice the people pointing and murmuring about the costumed character leaning out of the window next to the balcony.

Forty-Three

Joshua hesitated for a moment, but with everyone in the courtyard looking up, he took a deep breath, put a foot on the window sill and leapt six feet to the vine-covered stone wall. He surprised himself when he successfully grabbed the bunch of vines and found himself suspended above the ground.

The actor playing Romeo was angered. He sputtered some expletives that were not in the script.

Joshua lowered himself hand over hand as the people applauded below, thinking it was part of the show. When his feet touched the cobblestones, he turned and ran toward his mother.

He finally reached her. "Rainee! Rainee, am I glad to see you!"

She turned around, startled.

Joshua realized he still had his mask on and quickly removed it.

"Joshua!" she screamed, then pulled him into an embrace. "Oh my God! Your face! What did they do to you?"

Joshua looked away.

"Are you all right? How did you find me? Where are the men who took you?"

Joshua smiled. "Yep, I'm fine. If I had any doubt it was you, it's gone now."

She laughed and hugged him tightly. After losing him twice in her life, she was so glad to have him in her arms.

"Joshua, let me introduce you to Giulietta." He watched as the woman removed her mask and was shocked to see his former captor.

"Daisy! What are you doing here? How did you escape? Where did you go? Do the others know you're here?"

The girl hugged him, then stepped back. "My name is Giulietta, Joshua. I was never able to tell you."

He smiled at the ironies of their being in the Juliet castle and climbing down the vines to find Giulietta.

She continued. "There is great danger all around us. As you know, Tomasso and his men are here. We must find a place to hide until this is over. We cannot waste time."

But Tomasso had already spotted them. He recognized Joshua. The older woman must be Rainee Allen and— was that Giulietta? He could not believe his eyes. *Why is she here? That bitch came to save the kid! Well, that will not happen now!*

He raced toward the trio, then grabbed Giulietta by the arms, ready to punch her. "Puttana! You are here to save your Romeo? I knew you had a thing for him. I should kill you for interfering!"

Rainee was stunned and confused.

Joshua was equally shocked to see Tomasso at the very moment he found Rainee. The danger was real and the moment was now. He balled up his fist. With wild abandon, he threw a punch. It barely grazed Tomasso's cheek.

Tomasso let go of Giulietta and turned his attention to Joshua. He delivered a debilitating punch to the abdomen.

Joshua dropped. He lay on the ground, gasping for air.

Tomasso pulled a gun out of his pocket and pointed it at Joshua.

Rainee screamed, then lunged forward to grab his hand.

He squeezed the trigger and there was an explosion, but the bullet went wide.

As Tomasso tried to deflect Rainee, Giulietta dropped to the ground. Blood was spurting from her side.

Rainee cried out, "Help! Help! Someone get help!"

Chaos ensued. The crowd started running in every direction, women screaming, men grabbing their loved ones.

Fabrizio was suddenly there. He pointed a gun and yelled, "Put it down, Tomasso! Now!"

Tomasso hesitated. He looked at Fabrizio.

"I said put it down!"

It cannot finish this way! I need to get out of this! I need to get the money! She must know where it is! He turned, grabbed Rainee and put his gun to her head.

Joshua yelled, "Rainee!"

"Stay down, Josh! Stay down!" Rainee warned her son.

Fabrizio said, "Do not be stupid, Tomasso. Put the gun down. This will not end well. You know it. It is over. You need to come with me. Let her go and drop your gun."

Rainee's ears pricked up as the final piece of the puzzle fell into place. Fabrizio knew Tomasso.

Several other polizia arrived on the scene and encircled them. They all pointed their weapons at Tomasso. Some yelled for the few remaining onlookers to back away and move inside the castle.

Tomasso looked about frantically. "I will kill her! I will!" Retaining his hold on Rainee, he started backing away.

The police slowly opened a wide path for him.

"Put all your guns down! Down on the ground! Now! Do it now!"

Fabrizio said, "Tomasso, let Signora Allen go."

"I will not say it again! Put your weapons down, or she is dead!"

Fabrizio nodded to the officers. He ordered, "*Fai quello che dice.*"

Hesitatingly, they laid their weapons on the ground.

"There. You have got what you wanted. Now let her go!" commanded Fabrizio.

"No. I will take her with me for security. My security." He carefully turned them both around as he scanned the police, making certain he would be able to get away.

When Tomasso was half-turned with Rainee, Joshua saw an opportunity. He rolled over and picked up the police Beretta on the ground near him.

From the corner of her eye, Rainee saw his move. She cupped her right fist with her left hand and jabbed her elbow into Tomasso's abdomen.

Tomasso winced and loosened his grip.

Rainee ducked away.

Joshua fired.

The bullet hit Tomasso's thigh. He keeled over, dropping his gun.

Rainee quickly retrieved it and backed away from him.

The police surrounded him, and Fabrizio gently took the smoking gun from Joshua's trembling hands. He smiled. "Nice work."

Rainee ran to Joshua and they held each other.

The *Tecnico medico di emergenza* assessed and dressed Giulietta's wound, started an IV, and placed her onto a gurney. She told Joshua that she was scared and asked him if he would accompany her to the hospital. He nodded his head and turned to Rainee.

"Do you mind? Will you be alright?"

Rainee responded, "Of course. You go. I will be along as soon as we clear some things up here. Go. Be with her."

Fabrizio approached Rainee. "Rainee, where did you put the money? We have to find it."

"How well did you know the professor, Fabrizio?"

"*Scusami?*"

"You heard me. It was you I recognized in the picture. The one on the internet. The two of you together. And that man— Tomasso.

"No, Rainee. You misunderstood the situation."

She looked at him with distrust.

"He is my uncle. I was surprised to even see him here."

"Why didn't you mention your relationship back in Rome? There were plenty of opportunities. And this man named Tomasso? E5He was also the professor's nephew. Which makes him what, your brother?"

"No, a cousin. Look, you and Joshua have to give a statement. We can go to the local station and I will tell you everything. But where is the money? That is evidence in a crime scene."

"Aren't you curious where your uncle is?" She watched his face for any reaction.

"I saw him here. We spoke for a second and I asked him to leave. I assume he left."

"He's dead."

Fabrizio's face became ashen. "What?"

"I can bring you to where we left him. Giulietta hit him over the head with a rock. She saved my life. He was taking me to Juliet's tomb. He was going to take the money and kill me. She saved my life."

"*Dio Mio!* The money? No, that's not possible. He cannot be a part of this," Fabrizio said.

"I just said he was going to kill me in Juliet's tomb."

"I am so sorry, Rainee. I had no idea he was involved in all of this." He paused. "I suppose it could makes sense, though. He was with the Brigate Rosse a long time ago. But I thought that was all behind him."

"Well, apparently, kidnapping Joshua was his idea."

"Please, you have to bring me to his body."

"It's on the stairwell to the tomb. As far as the money, I will take you to it, but only with several of your men. I'm not ready to trust you."

"Si, I understand."

When they arrived at the stairwell to Juliet's tomb, Rainee froze and pointed. "He was right there! We were sure he was dead!"

The only remaining proof that the professor had been there was a blood-stained rock and the blood seeping into the cobble-stoned ground. The police collected it for DNA evidence.

All of them followed her to the kitchen to retrieve the money from inside the urn. With the officers by her side, Rainee pointed to the urn. One of them reached inside.

It was empty.

Forty-Four

The hospital hallway was long, sterile white and had the familiar faint smell of antiseptic. Empty gurneys lined the walls. Joshua found a phone and called Ricky.

"Dad? Hi Dad!"

"Joshua! Oh my God! It's so good to hear your voice! Are you hurt? You've been through an awful ordeal. It was so painful not knowing what was going on. Not being there to help."

"I'm okay, Dad, thanks to Rainee and this girl I met. Rainee was amazing. She didn't give up searching for me for a minute. She's pretty incredible!"

Ricky responded. "I know. She's a pretty awesome woman."

"Dad, you gave them the money? I am so sorry. They're still looking for it, but I don't know if they'll find it."

"Joshua, don't worry about that. All I care about is that you're safe and sound. I was so scared! Your mother and I have been beside ourselves worrying about you. She'll be so disappointed that she wasn't here when you called. I know she wants to talk with you. She just wants to hear your voice."

"I'd love to hear her's, too. Please tell Mom I love her. I'm so glad you're doing better. I can't get into it now, Dad, but I promise I will call you soon to tell you more about what happened. But no need to worry anymore. All is well! I can't wait to see you soon. Take care, Dad. I love you!"

"I love you too, son. So much."

They each hung up.

Detective Piscitelli finished his initial paperwork with Rainee at the local police station and drove her to the hospital.

He escorted her to the waiting room where Joshua was sitting tapping his foot impatiently. So relieved to see Rainee, he stood as soon as she entered.

She hugged her son, then asked, "Are you all right? How badly were you hurt? Did the doctors examine you? How is Giulietta?"

"Everything's good with me, Rainee. The doctors examined me. Nothing's broken. I am sore, but that's about it. At least I wasn't shot. But poor Giulietta, I hope she's going to be okay. They haven't told me anything yet."

Rainee hugged him again and settled into one of the uncomfortable waiting room chairs. There were a few other families in the large room, each occupying their own section. One man lay splayed across three chairs fast asleep. A television was hung in a corner. The volume was kept low and no one was watching. It was time that she called Martin to let him know she was alright.

"Martin? Oh, Honey, it's so good to hear your voice!"

"Rainee, were you injured? Joshua?"

"No, we're okay. There was a shooting, but both of us are fine and, well—" She stopped talking, choked up and sobbed.

"Oh, my love, I'm so sorry. What can I do?"

"Nothing. I'm sorry I'm crying. I guess it's just a delayed reaction to a horrible experience. Really, we're fine. It just didn't go as smoothly as planned. But the bottom line is that I am with Joshua and he's safe. He really went through an unbelievably difficult ordeal."

"I have never been so worried. But you're all right and that's all that matters. So, what happened? Can you tell me?"

"Well, it's quite a long story. I will share it with you soon, but we have some business to attend to here. I just wanted to let you know that both of us are safe and sound. I promise I'll tell you all about it. I should go now, but I'll call you later in the evening, when I have some privacy. I love you."

They sat together; neither said a word. Rainee looked over and took Joshua's hand. They relished the quiet and reflected on the past several days. Announcements over the intercom intermittently pierced the silence. A doctor in scrubs eventually entered the room and called for Joshua Greenberg.

The surgeon reported, to their relief, that the surgery went well. They had removed a single bullet, which had nicked Giulietta's spleen. The splenic trauma caused her to lose a lot of blood, but the surgeons now had that under control. She would need to stay in the hospital for a several days to recover.

Fabrizio returned to the waiting area in time to hear the doctor tell them that Giulietta would have to stay for a while.

He told Rainee and Joshua that he had already arranged to have an armed guard outside her door around the clock for as long as necessary. There was no telling how many participants of the Brigate Rosse were still around. "Their plot may have fallen apart, but Giulietta took part in it. She knew these men and she betrayed them. They could seek revenge." He paused. "You must also understand, Joshua, that when she is released, she will have to stand trial."

"But she saved Rainee. She told me she hated Tomasso. And she helped me in my escape. She could easily have knocked out Rainee and taken the money. She didn't."

"I believe all that. It will be in my report to the judge, and perhaps he will consider that in his decision. However, she was part of the group when they planned your kidnapping and held you in captivity. And we have to take into consideration that she still might be working with the professor. He is missing, and maybe that knock on the head was staged for Rainee's sake to make her believe she was helping her. It could not have been too hard. After all, he did not stay unconscious. We just do not know enough yet."

Rainee's eyes narrowed. "No, the whole story has not been revealed. Not yet. There are many questions remaining. But I have no doubt the truth will come out."

"Since Giulietta is still in recovery, Joshua, I would like you to come to the station to make your statement while it is fresh in your minds. You can return here later."

Joshua said, "I want to stay here. Just in case. Believe me, I can't forget the past week even if I tried."

Fabrizio shook his head and sighed. "Then I will have to send an officer here to take your statement. Can we get you some food from the cafeteria?"

Rainee shook her head. "I think I want to go back to the hotel to freshen up. We'll eat there. Thank you anyway."

He left them alone.

"You know, Joshua, we do have some time now while Giulietta is resting. Why don't we take a taxi back to my hotel and get you a room? There's even a shop in the hotel. I bet we could get you some clothes to change into."

"Yeah, I must reek."

"Not too bad. We can clean up, then grab some food and come back here later. What do you say?"

They pulled up to the front of the hotel when Rainee realized that she had left her purse in the room safe. She told the driver, he nodded and told her to hurry back with the fare.

Entering the hotel, Joshua exclaimed, "Oh my God! Those bastards have my wallet with my driver's license in it. The rest of my stuff, including my passport, my clothes, my laptop, and even my souvenirs are all back at my hotel in Rome! I hope they didn't think I skipped out on the room bill!"

They stared at each other and simultaneously broke into laughter. It was just a shared moment of silliness, or maybe a little hysteria. The tension that had been forged over a week of panic-filled terror was released.

"Good thought, Joshua. We'll call them soon to let them know you didn't stiff them and will be back to reclaim your stuff as soon as we can. Meanwhile, let's get you some clothes," said Rainee.

While he was in the shop, Rainee checked Joshua into a room just a few doors down from hers. They agreed they would first shower, then meet in the lobby to get some food.

She opened her room door, walked in, and was pleasantly surprised to see the room back in order. All the furniture was in place, no phone lines were running across the floor, and the ashtrays were gone. Unfortunately, the air still had the lingering smell of stale tobacco.

Rainee took her time in the shower. She turned on the shower and let the hot water wash away the tension from the past week.

Joshua was waiting in the lobby when Rainee arrived. "How do you feel, Joshua?"

"Boy, I can honestly say I really needed that. I feel great. Clean again."

She smiled and responded, "Me, too! But I have to say you did look dashing in your Romeo costume. Torn tights and all."

He laughed as they walked into the hotel restaurant.

It was an off-hour, so it was not busy. The white table cloths, shiny flatware, and fresh cut, colorful flowers on each table created an elegant atmosphere.

The maître d' showed them to a table, handed them menus and asked what they would like to drink.

Rainee said, "I could use a drink. You?"

Joshua nodded. "Oh yeah, I'd love a beer. Can I have a Peroni, please?"

"Make mine a glass of Pinot Grigio, thank you."

After they ordered their food, Rainee's thoughts turned to her son. *What must he be thinking right now? Do I wait for him, or do I approach the elephant in the room? Is now even the time?*

"Rainee?"

"Yes, Joshua?"

She thought that he was ready to ask her and braced for the inevitable.

"Can I ask you something?"

Okay, here it comes. "Sure, ask me anything."

"I've been wondering about this since I was a kid."

"Uh huh."

"What... what kind of name is Rainee?"

Rainee laughed with relief.

"Oh, I'm sorry," Joshua quickly said.

"Oh no, it's okay. Believe me, I'm used to it." She chuckled. "Here's the story. My mother— your grandmother— was very pregnant with me and due any day. By the way, I can't wait for you to meet them. They're going to love you. Anyway, it was February. It had been raining nonstop for days. My mom had cabin fever. My dad— your grandfather— suggested they go see a movie. It was *Raintree County*. Do you know the movie? Liz Taylor, Montgomery Clift."

Joshua shook his head.

"It's an old one. Anyhow, they arrived at the theater and it was still raining. The marquis displayed the movie title, with two letters missing. I'm sure you can guess which letters. T and R. So, it spelled out Rain ee County. While they were watching the movie, my mother's water broke. They laughed between the contractions because it was raining, *and* my mother was too."

Joshua laughed.

"It seems they thought it was appropriate to name me after a movie title that was missing a couple of letters. And this was all before the hippie era began, when kids were named Moonfrye and Dharma. I suppose you could say they were ahead of their time."

"Moonfrye? Really?" Joshua nodded. "That's a great story."

Joshua paused, looking down at his hands which were folded together on the table.

She studied his face for a moment. "You have Ricky's eyes. Did you know that?"

"Dad always said I had your eyes."

"Really?"

He looked up. "I was wondering how I can thank you."

"Thank me? I should thank you. For coming back into my life. It was you who initiated the call."

"Sure, but you didn't have to want to meet me."

"Oh, but I did. Right from the beginning."

"What do you mean?" Joshua's right eyebrow raised, the way Ricky's used to.

"Ahem!" The waiter interrupted to place their drinks. Then stood poised, pen and pad in hand, to take their order.

The moment of interruption gave Rainee time to recapture her thoughts. The ordered their meal.

She continued, "You know I agreed to give you up. After your birth, they brought you to me and I fell in love, right then. But I knew I would not be a good mother at such a young age. I wanted a career. I wanted a life. Ricky and I had agreed—" She stopped. "But you've heard this story."

"Sort of, but not from you. Do you mind if I ask you some more questions?"

"Sure."

He took his time.

She waited.

Finally, he said, "I've thought about this moment all my life. If we ever met, what would I say to you? What would you say to me? How would I answer?"

He played with his fork. "I think the first question is why you gave me up?"

Rainee looked into his eyes. "I was a senior in college. I didn't want a child to be a burden to me— and yes, that is the word I used then— a burden. But you must understand the times. It was 1978 and women were coming into their own. Women's lib and all. I wanted to establish a career and experience life. Be free to do what I wanted to do. Having a baby was not in my plans. But your father was insistent. He lectured me. He pontificated. He talked and talked—"

"Yeah, that sounds like Dad."

"Well, he wore me down. He said *he* would raise you, and I agreed. As you know, after graduation, he moved with you across the country. And sadly, that was the end of a great friendship. You know, losing Ricky's friendship almost killed me. Anyway, you were taken from my arms one week after your birth."

Tears filled Rainee's eyes. "I didn't know you, sweetie. When I think of what I missed, I... I want to say I'm sorry. I hope you can accept my apology. I hope we can have a relationship. You're an amazing young man. I'm so proud of you."

Joshua said, "I've wanted to meet you for years, but I didn't have the courage. I thought you might turn me away. I'm glad we did meet. Okay, the circumstances could've been better. *A lot* better!"

They both laughed, letting loose the apprehension that had hung in the air. "Can I meet my sister Jana?"

"Oh my God, yes. She would love to meet you. And Martin too. And you have a grandmother and an aunt in London. And an ocean of family back in Massachusetts. They would all love to meet you."

"Did you ever regret your decision?"

Rainee hesitated. Her mood saddened. "Well, yes. About four years after you were born, I called your dad. Not to take you back. I had no right. But just to get in touch with my old friend and to find out about you and what you were like."

"What happened?"

Rainee held up one hand. "Nothing against your dad. I will always have a special place in my heart for him."

"But?"

"Well, he told me a little about his work, but he didn't think it was appropriate to talk about you. And I understood. Really I did."

"Oh."

"Joshua, maybe I shouldn't have said anything. It's just that there has been so much emotion in me this past week, I'm not thinking clearly. Ricky was absolutely right then. And I knew it."

"Still, that must've had an effect on you."

"Well, yeah, sure. By then I was about twenty-six years old. Still single. No boyfriend. I was down, and a bit depressed. I really felt regret giving you up. I felt a terrible guilt. I hit rock bottom. Not with drink or drugs or anything like that. I was just depressed and feeling anguished."

"I'm so sorry, Rainee."

"Don't be. Please, don't be. I saw a therapist and she explained that I was going through a mourning period. Same as when a person dies. You see, I lost a piece of me when Ricky left with you. It just took a few years to catch up to me. When the therapist explained that, I felt lighter, and I finally understood my emotions. Then life got easier. I began to enjoy myself again. And of course, years later when I gave birth to my exquisite little girl, I felt my life was complete."

Rainee continued. "Joshua, I am *so* grateful that you called me. You know, after your call, feelings that were left unheeded and fermenting came to the surface. I *needed* to meet you. I realized that I had an open wound that needed healing. You healed me, Joshua. Thank you."

"Wish I had known all that."

"How could you? Please don't ever blame yourself. Or your dad. Not for any of it. Not for one second. I'm just glad that we are here. Together. Now. And hopefully, forever."

They paused and her thoughts turned to Giulietta. She asked what their relationship was and why he cared about someone who had been involved with the kidnappers.

Joshua explained how she helped him escape. Then he questioned, "But was it all part of a plot? Was Piscitelli right to suspect that she used me like the professor did?"

Joshua was pensive for a moment. "You know, Rainee, I have mixed feelings about Giulietta. She certainly was a willing participant in my kidnapping and was part of the plan to ransom me for Dad's money, at least at first. I saw no difference between her and the men when I was first taken, but over the course of a couple of days, that started to change."

Rainee sat up straighter and nodded. "Go on."

"She was kinder to me than the others. She held my hand when I got emotional. We even hugged on more than one occasion. It was weird. You know, I even thought I was falling for her a little. She was kind to me when the others were incredibly cruel."

Rainee said. "I can understand how those things could happen, Joshua. You were in survival mode. It sounds like that could be a survival strategy for any hostage. Giulietta probably felt bad for you and your situation, too. She may have even started to have feelings for you, as well. That can definitely happen between people on opposite sides of a hostage situation. It seems obvious that you both started to feel bad for each other."

Joshua responded, "Yeah. It's true. She felt bad for me, but I really felt bad for her, too. I witnessed her being treated like a dog. I saw Tomasso beat her. He punched and slapped her, and his verbal abuse was in some ways even worse than the physical abuse. I was scared for her. I definitely felt bad."

"Not surprising," Rainee responded.

"As I told you, I'm pretty sure she even helped me escape when I ran that night. I don't know that for sure, but I think she intentionally didn't lock the door when she went up to bed that night. I never did ask her, but I'm pretty sure. I think I'll ask her when I can.

As far as whether she used me like Professor Esposito did, I really don't think she did. I believe she was just in the wrong place at the wrong time with the wrong crowd. No doubt she was attracted to the money, but I don't think she thought it out. It was temporary excitement, but then the reality of it hit her. Anyway, that's what I think."

Rainee smiled. "All I know is, I'm so happy and thankful you are here with me, and that you're all right. I can't bear the thought that they beat you, but it's behind you now. You have your mom and dad and me who are thankful for you and who will give you endless hugs forever."

Rainee watched Joshua finish his spaghetti and meatballs, focaccia bread, soda, and a dessert. She played with her beef carpaccio salad and downed three glasses of water. She had not realized how thirsty she was.

Finally, Joshua pushed back his chair and patted his belly. "I'm full. Finally."

His mother smiled with satisfaction. "Drink some water, Joshua. You could easily be dehydrated."

He looked at her, with an okay-Mom-you're-right kind of smile and nodded. "True." He swallowed two glasses of water.

It was finally all out in the open. Joshua asked more questions and Rainee answered them truthfully and happily. Conversation streamed easily between the two.

Rainee went to her room to retrieve the laptop the police left behind for her to borrow. Then they took a taxi back to the hospital to check on Giulietta. She was awake and sitting up.

"How are you feeling? You look good!"

"Thank you, Joshua. I am a bit— how you say?— foggy, but better now. Thanks to pain drugs. How are you, Rainee?"

Rainee smiled and said, "I'm fine! I'm just happy to hear that you're doing better." She smiled and reached out to hold Giulietta's hand.

They were engaged in some small talk, when Fabrizio entered the hospital room.

"Hello, Giulietta. I see you're feeling better."

She nodded, but her face suddenly turned sullen.

"Joshua, Rainee, I need to speak with you out in the hall, please." They followed him out of the room.

"We still need your statements. I am sending someone to take them soon."

He hesitated. "My uncle was spotted in Rome. I am headed there immediately."

Joshua stood up. "That's my dad's money. I want to be there to help!"

"I'm sorry, Joshua," Fabrizio said. "That's not possible. I won't allow it. You could still be in danger and we do not know if the Brigate Rosse has other members who might try to retaliate. You would put not only yourself, but my men in danger. I simply cannot allow you to be part of this investigation."

He paused and looked at Rainee, knowing he was going to come up against opposition. "You must stay here, too, Rainee. You can watch over the girl and your son. I am sorry. I will need you both to stay here and answer any questions that come up."

He turned and left.

Rainee said, "Ha! He thinks I'm going to sit back and let them—" She made air quotes with her fingers, "—'investigate'. There is more going on here and we need to involve Interpol. Joshua, I do agree with him in one way, though. You stay with Giulietta. She will need you and I won't be gone long. Maybe a few days, but I'll call you five times a day! Ten times a day! I won't take a chance of losing you again!"

They spent the next couple of hours catching up with more details of each other's lives. Late that afternoon, Officer Domenico Ansari came to the waiting room to take their preliminary statements. It took over two hours before he was satisfied that he had enough information to bring back to his boss.

As he was leaving, he told both of them that more thorough questioning might be necessary and to stay reachable and in the area for at least a week.

Forty-Five

Rainee received the call from Fabrizio barely ten minutes after Officer Ansari left. "I wanted to let you know we found out the professor went to Venice, not Rome. He bought a train ticket with a credit card, so it was easy to find out where he went."

Rainee felt a tinge of hope. *Venice. I'll be on my way there by tonight.*

"Remember what I said, Rainee. You are not to get involved with this. Let the police handle this. You do understand, si?"

"Of course," she answered. "Go do your police work. In fact, do anything you have to, but get the money back."

"I am sending a team to find him and bring him back."

"You're not going?" she asked.

"No. I cannot. I have been called back to Rome. Do not worry, though. My men will find him and bring him to Rome to stand trial."

"But what—" She thought it strange he was not going considering his relationship to the professor. "Okay. I understand." She grinned as she said goodbye.

"Joshua, that was Fabrizio, and he told me they think the professor is on his way to Venice. He apparently bought a train ticket with a credit card."

He nodded, but seemed lost in thought. "You know, the professor is no dummy. He probably bought that ticket to throw them off the trail. Why would he use a credit card when he has all that cash? He may be going somewhere else. He's kind of wily like that."

"Wily, eh? You think so? But where else would he go?"

"Well, I was thinking about that. One night while we were in the hotel having supper, he kept going on about a childhood friend he had in Rome. He said they had grown up together and kept in touch throughout their lives. He had planned to spend a few days together with him after the conference. Do you think he could have contacted him and gone to his apartment in Rome?"

"I don't know, but it sounds like it's worth following up. I find it odd that Fabrizio is not headed to Venice. He said he's going to Rome. Did the professor say his friend's name during your chat?"

"He did, but I'm not sure I can remember. We were both drinking and I was feeling a little tipsy. Let me think."

Rainee felt like the lead was worth following up, but how to start? Without a name, she had nothing. "Do you think you might remember it if we talk about the conversation for a while? Do you remember a first name?"

He couldn't remember at all.

"Rainee, I just can't think of it. We need your laptop. Maybe we can find a... wait a minute... Paolo! Yes, Paolo! That's it! Paolo!"

It was a start.

The last name was longer in coming, but after a full hour of trying to remember, Joshua yelled out, "Milani! His last name was Milani. Paolo Milani. I remembered because when the professor told me his name, I said to him that it sounded like 'Milan' and I had always wanted to visit Milan! That's it, Rainee! It's Paolo Milani in Rome. Can you look up his address?"

"I can try, Josh. Great going!" She opened the laptop, waited for it to start up. It only took Rainee just a few minutes before she came up with three address listings for Paolo Milani. She wrote them down.

Rainee said, "I want to call these numbers. Maybe we will get lucky."

She dialed a number, but it was not a working number. When she dialed the second number, a male voice answered, "Pronto!"

Rainee quickly said, "I am calling with a message for Paolo Milani. This is Professor Esposito's secretary."

"Professor who?"

"Esposito. He wanted to confirm his upcoming visit with him."

"Signora, I *am* Paolo and I have no idea what you are talking about. Maledetti venditori! Always calling when I am eating..." His voice trailed off and Rainee heard a click.

"Well, he sounded pretty sincere."

She tried the last number and let it ring for a long time unanswered. "I think— or at least, hope— we have our address. We are making huge assumptions here. But, I think it is worth a try."

"I'm going with you."

"No, Josh. Stay and be with Giulietta when she wakes up. She will need you. Besides, it would be particularly dangerous for you to be there. Don't forget, there are still a bunch of Brigate Rosse members on the loose."

"Okay, if you say so." He agreed, a bit relieved. However, when Rainee went to the restroom, he copied the Milani address onto a napkin.

Forty-Six

The wait to board the one-hour flight from Verona to Rome was longer than the actual flight. It gave Rainee the opportunity to call Martin. He was nearly apoplectic when she briefed him on what had transpired in Verona. She was able to calm him as she told him the story.

The hard part was relating to him what she was about to do.

"Are you out of your mind? No! No, Rainee. Don't be a hero. You have your son. Forget about the bloody money."

"Martin, Honey, I'm not trying to be a hero. But I have a gut feeling that Detective Piscitelli is corrupt."

"So what? Let it be. You're putting yourself in danger yet again." Rainee could hear Martin mumble something about having to sit down.

"Calm down, Martin. Please, Honey, calm down."

"Really? That's easy for you to say. I am coming to Rome."

"Look, Rome is a big city. He'll never see me. I have contacted the Interpol agent I talked with before. Remember, Piscitelli sent them away. But as soon as I told them I may have evidence of corruption they wanted to meet with me in their Rome office. Plus, I have a lead, too. A name. A connection to the professor."

Martin let out a long sigh. "I know you, my love. You're going to get yourself embroiled in this mess. You'll see it to the end."

"No, Martin. I'll inform Interpol about every little detail. Then I'll leave it in their hands."

"You promise?"

Attempting to avoid making a promise she might not be able to keep, Rainee laughed. "Hey, maybe they'll turn it over to MI-6, and I'll get to meet Agent 007. Bond. James Bond."

"There she goes again. You have your next book in your head, don't you?"

"If they make this one into a movie too, we'll vacation at that hotel in Venice. The whole family, including Joshua."

"Bugger and blast! It'll be just the two of us, my love. We are surrounded by family in this house. I want you all to myself for a change."

Rainee laughed at the resolve in his voice. "Yes, Martin. That's a great idea. Just the two of us."

"You didn't give me that promise."

The airport was announcing that her flight was about to begin boarding.

"Oh, that's my flight. I'll call you from Rome."

"I love you, Rainee."

"I love you more." She powered down her cell phone and boarded her short flight to the Eternal City.

Forty-Seven

Joshua couldn't sleep even though the hotel bed was incredibly comfortable. He finally got up, showered and dressed, so that he could return to the hospital to check on Giulietta. The past ten days had taken their toll on him. He was anxious. It wasn't over, not yet. He was concerned about Rainee. She was still involved, and he was worried that she might find herself in trouble.

Fabrizio called him several times to see if he was all right, but Joshua knew he was calling to make sure that he and Rainee stayed put while the police were trying to find the professor. Each time he asked for Rainee, Joshua made up some excuse. He said that she went out to pick some food up or was on the phone. He suspected Fabrizio did not believe him, and with each call, he promised he would have Rainee call him.

Joshua left several voice messages with her but he had not heard back. Of course, she'd left only yesterday. Maybe she was busy with Interpol. Maybe she was out casing the addresses to find out which one housed the professor.

Where was she? Why hadn't she returned his calls? She said she would call. Was she hurt? His mind wandered as he worried about her. Finally, he thought, *I'm going to go to Rome. Will I even find her there?*

He checked his pockets. He had only €200 in bills. Rainee had given him the money so he would have some walking-around money. Would it be enough for a train ticket to Rome?

What if I can't contact her before I get there? I don't even know the name of the hotel she booked. But, I do have the Milani address. He took the elevator down to the concierge to ask for help in obtaining a ticket.

"Signore, would you be able to help me find out how much a train ticket to Rome would be? And what the schedule is?"

"Ah, yes. Good morning, Mr. Greenberg. I hope you had a pleasant sleep," the concierge said with a smile. "I can certainly help you find that information. Just a moment while I make a call to *Stazione Termini.*"

Joshua nodded and looked around the lobby. He waited while the concierge dialed the number.

His gaze followed an attractive young woman as she walked toward the front entrance of the hotel. To his horror, he saw Fabrizio enter and hold the door for her. He suddenly froze and turned away. He waited nervously, hoping Fabrizio would not see him. It didn't work.

"Joshua, I came to talk with Rainee, since she has not returned my calls. Where is she? I want to see her. Now."

"Ahh, she's out. I think she said she was going to get her nails done." His response sounded weak, but it was the best he could muster on the spot.

"Look, I know you are covering for her and I know she is not here, so you are going to tell me where she went. And you are going to tell me now!" Fabrizio leaned in intimidatingly, towering over Joshua's five foot, nine inch height.

Joshua offered a cautious response. "I'm not really sure. She said she was going out and when I asked where, she told me she needed air. So, I really don't know."

"Joshua, this not a game. You are obstructing an investigation. You must tell me."

"Look, she gave your department all of the information you required. She's free to go wherever she wants. You have no right to harass her! Besides, you said you were headed to Rome. Why are you here?"

"Two things. I wanted to let her know that we found out that they called back the men from the Brigate Rosse from England. Her family can now return to their home. She will be happy about that. Second, and most important, I want to protect her. Do you know if she went to Venezia? I told her not to go. If you care about her, you need to tell me where she went. I have knowledge that she may be in imminent danger. There are people hunting for her. You have to tell me. If you do not, she could get killed. You do not want that, do you, Joshua? You do not want to be responsible for her getting killed, do you?"

"Killed?" Joshua asked, shaken. *Shit! Do I tell him where she is? He may be lying, but do I take a chance with her life? I can't. I'll tell him and try to contact her to warn her.* "Okay. Okay, I'll tell you. She went to Rome."

"Rome? Why would she go to Rome?" He took another step toward Joshua, who instinctively stepped back. "I told her that the professor was in Venezia!"

His sudden outburst caught Joshua off guard. "I don't know." He answered sheepishly. "She said she had a hunch."

"Okay, Joshua." The detective took a deep breath. "Do you know where she is staying? There is still a chance that we may be able to save her if I get to her first. Do you know?"

"No. No, I really don't."

Forty-Eight

The view from her balcony at the Hotel Ponte Lunetto was of St. Peter's Basilica. The suite was clean, but too modern for her taste. Decorated with all white furniture, the only thing black in the room was the television screen and a leather sofa. Even the newly cut flowers were white roses. Rainee looked at the four-poster bed and wished Martin were with her. But she intended this to be a fast trip.

Rainee realized she had not powered up her cell phone. She rummaged through her purse to locate it. She felt bad that she had let time go by without calling Joshua, especially after seeing how many voice messages he had left.

Her call to him proved to be alarming. He informed her about Piscitelli's insistent push for information and that, fearing for her life, Joshua had revealed to the detective that she was in Rome.

"Well, it's good you don't know the name of my hotel then. The less you know, the safer you will be."

"I really didn't like what he said. Please be careful, Rainee. It's hard to know who to trust."

"Interpol. I believe I can trust them."

She had registered as R. Wagner, her married name. If Detective Piscitelli was on the lookout for her, he would probably be searching for Rainee Allen.

Knowing that the Red Brigade had her old phone number, she had tossed it and purchased a new phone at the airport. She gave Joshua the new number.

The bathtub looked inviting, so Rainee kicked off her shoes, grabbed a bathrobe and prepared a bath with the bath salts provided by the hotel. While the tub was filling, she called Martin to give him the new number. She had to leave the information with his front desk, as he was seeing patients. But she kept the cell phone plugged in next to the bed and let the hot water relax her tense muscles. Rainee had not realized how tight her body had become with all the stresses of the past week. This bath felt like heaven and she let out a long, sigh, accompanied with, "Ahhhhh. Just what I needed."

The phone rang, waking Rainee with a jolt. She had fallen asleep in the tub. "Damn!" She grabbed a towel and not wanting to slip, carefully walked on the ceramic tile to the phone. Too late. It stopped ringing. "Dammit. Must have been Martin."

She was just about to pick up her phone to call him back, when the phone rang a second time.

"Ciao, amore mio," she said in a sultry tone.

"Is this Rainee Allen?" The unfamiliar voice surprised her.

"Who is this?"

"Agent Stock. I'm with Interpol, ma'am."

"How did you—" Rainee stopped herself, realizing what organization she was dealing with.

"I want to confirm some facts before your appointment with us later this afternoon."

"Certainly, Agent."

"You claim to have proof that the Red Brigade is operating and being led by an Italian detective."

"Well, I am confident that a faction of the original Red Brigade is operating."

"So, you are of the opinion—"

"Not an opinion, sir. I have what may be actual proof. Agent Stock, have you been made aware that my son, Joshua Greenberg, was kidnapped and held for ransom for five million Euros?"

"Yes, ma'am. I have the folder in front of me. Detective Piscitelli oversaw that operation." Rainee could hear him rustling pages.

"Correct. Are you aware that we got Joshua back? The money, however, is still missing."

"Yes, ma'am."

"I believe I know who ran this operation, and quite possibly, where to locate him."

"That will be most helpful. I can send a car to pick you up shortly. Where are you located?"

Once again, Rainee's heightened instinctual sense rang out like a church bell. *Why ask these questions now, and not in the station? Am I being setup by Fabrizio?*

"Agent Stock, Interpol handles organized crimes and corruption, true?"

"Uh, yes, ma'am."

"Just confirming what I already knew. I will be in your department at the appointed time. I... uh... have some shopping I want to do first. Will I meet you there?"

"No. Um... no, ma'am. I will be on a different assignment."

"I see. Well then, thank you. Goodbye." Rainee hung up before he could say goodbye. She hoped the call had not been traced but feared she could not take that chance.

Joshua had told her that he revealed to Fabrizio that she was in Rome. *He could have had an officer waiting at the airport. But, Stock didn't know which hotel. Perhaps, if I had been followed, they got lost in Rome's crazy traffic.*

She quickly dressed, packed her clothes, and left the hotel through a back entrance.

Taking a side alley, she emerged onto a busy street and hailed a taxi. She gave the driver the address Interpol Agent Harrington had given her.

Why wait? Might as well get there early. If Fabrizio did know she was in Rome, she had better move fast, or he and the professor would be gone quickly.

Once inside the impressive marble building, Rainee asked several people for Agent Stock. No one seemed to know him, but she reasoned that it was a big department. She followed signs to the office where her afternoon appointment was to be held. She spoke to the receptionist and inquired about Agent Stock. The young woman with fire-red hair responded that there was no agent by that name, at least, not in the Rome office.

Rainee dug through her purse and came up with Agent Harrington's business card. She handed it to the receptionist.

"Oh, certainly. You do have an appointment with Agent Harrington. Bit early though."

So I was right to be alarmed. "Yes, I know my appointment isn't for a few hours. But I had reason to believe I was in danger, so I came here straightaway."

"I will let him know. Please have a seat." The red-head's Cockney accent was a welcomed accent after spending so much time around Italians.

Agent Harrington returned with the receptionist. "Thank you, Enola." He held out his hand to Rainee. "Pleased to see you again, Ms. Allen. Won't you follow me? Here, allow me." He carried her luggage into his office.

"Coffee? Espresso?"

"Tea, please."

He nodded to Enola.

His office felt spartan to her. The walls were devoid of any certificates, posters, or pictures. Just a desk, file cabinet, computer, telephone, and several wooden chairs lined up against the wall. He took one and placed it opposite his desk chair.

"Enola said you felt you were in danger. Please tell me everything."

She worked her story backward, starting with the odd call from an Agent Stock, which had raised her suspicions. She revealed the events of the past two weeks.

Detective Harrington took notes and recorded the session. She noted he used a fountain pen, like her husband did. But unlike Martin, this detective was left-handed, and she marveled how the ink did not smear.

She needed to stand and pace as she related her story. The detective was patient as she paused at times to make sure she had the events in the correct order.

It took her a full hour from start to finish.

Then she asked, "And what about this fictitious Agent Stock from Interpol? Is it possible one of the Brigate Rosse spotted me?"

"Quite possible. But you said he asked where you were staying. That tells me they don't know which hotel you are in. Just the same, it's good you brought your things. I would advise changing hotels in case they were able to trace the call. And I will then station an agent with you."

"Will you be staking out Milani's place? It's possible Esposito is hiding there with the money."

Harrington nodded, with a look that projected: "obviously."

Rainee calmed down a little and took a sip of her tea, which was now cold.

"I promise you that we will be looking into all that you have told me. If he had any inkling that we are on to him, he would run. It must be handled, shall we say, delicately. Wait too long and the money— the proof— will be gone. And so will he. Besides, we do need to find out if the Milani address you narrowed it down to is the right one. That will be done immediately."

Agent Harrington put down his pen. "I understand that this had been bloody difficult for you. Quite a turn of events. You go to Venice to meet your son and end up chasing him down to save him."

Rainee sighed. "Yes, not exactly the holiday we had planned. I'm just happy he is safe now."

"Ms. Allen, why don't I have some lunch brought up? You have certainly earned a break. In the meanwhile, I will bring my colleagues up-to-date. You may use my office."

"Thank you. Now that you mention it, I am famished."

One hour later, a more relaxed Rainee sat quietly in the office unhurriedly finishing her lunch. Ricky was healing, Joshua and Giulietta were under police protection, Interpol was involved, and she could finally see the light at the end of this long, dark, and miserable tunnel. Soon she would be in her London home with her family. She would introduce her son to them. Little Jana would be overjoyed at having a big brother.

Then she and Joshua would fly to California together and he would be reunited with his family. She hoped she and Ricky would renew the friendship she once cherished.

Rainee relaxed for the first time in what felt like a very long time.

Forty-Nine

Joshua told Giulietta what Fabrizio said. "What do you think? Do you think Rainee could really be in trouble?"

"I do, Joshua. These men will not stop. I am sure there are several of the Brigade members in Rome now, looking for her and for Esposito. They will want to get the money back from Esposito, who double-crossed them, and they will want to find Rainee to punish her for screwing up the whole plan with you. I am sure they are there already."

Joshua had no idea what to do. "I have already warned her." he said. "She is so tenacious. She won't give up. Rainee will see it to the end." He shook his head. "I want to be there to protect her, but I don't know where she's staying."

Giulietta reached for Joshua's hand. "I know. It is frustrating, but she will be all right. I just know it." She squeezed his hand and he squeezed back.

"We have been through a lot. Joshua, tell me about your life. Tell me about you and Rainee."

He took a deep breath and then related his life's story, all the way to meeting Rainee for the first time, and their long heart-to-heart in the waiting room.

"Dio Mio? Are you telling me the truth?"

"I know. I can hardly believe it myself. My dad was always very respectful of her. He never had a bad word to say about her. In fact, he encouraged me to read her books and even took me to the movie that was made based on her first novel."

"Really? I did not know she was a writer! That is wonderful! Wow! You have two famous parents! Everyone knows who your father is, of course. The world knows. How exciting!"

"Yeah. Dad's special. When I was small, he used to take me to baseball games at Candlestick Park in San Francisco. He made a lot of time for me then. Those were great days for me. I will never forget them."

He was quiet for a moment. "You know, I thought about that a lot when I was being held in that first house they brought me to. I really thought I might die. It was incredibly scary and lonely. You were the only person who was even a little nice to me. You made it as tolerable as it could be. Thank you."

"You are welcome, Joshua. That was a difficult time for me, because being a kidnapper is not who I am. In fact, it's the very opposite. I think of myself as kind, maybe even gentle. But I was going with Tomasso. I still cannot believe I thought he was nice! He somehow made me trust him. He is a... a... *mostro*. That is it. You know *mostro*? Monster, in English, I think."

Joshua nodded. He felt terrible for her. "Yes. I know. He's a bastard. I hope he's put away in prison for a long, long time."

"*Anch'io*. Me too," she whispered. "I know I will have to face jail time for my part in the kidnapping and it is scaring the hell out of me. I do not know if I can do it."

He understood that she was just caught up in the plan of the others.

On the other hand, she did sign on to steal Dad's money. This is difficult. I like her, but in some sense she is still an enemy. Shit.

Maybe he could help her by testifying that she resisted the plan as soon as it started.

Fifty

Time at the Interpol department did not move fast enough for Rainee. They had agreed to move on the information she supplied, but she watched people moving in what felt like slow motion. Impatient, she hovered over one agent's desk, and then another, making them uncomfortable enough to get up and move. Just as she planned. This gave her an opportunity to get a glance at the computer screens. Most monitors did not offer any information on the case. She hoped to spot just one.

Seeing her coming toward him, one flustered agent moved away from his desk as soon as Rainee caught his eye. She tried not to smile, but a slight, satisfying grin escaped her. Rainee covered her grin with her hand and quickly looked away.

This particular monitor had Esposito's mug shot in the top right corner. Information on the current and past Red Brigade plastered the left side of the monitor. But what really caught her eye was the picture of Milani's apartment building. There was an address and phone number. *Bingo!* she thought. Rainee peered at it, then quickly walked away from the desk.

She was satisfied that it was the same address she had given them.

Agent Harrington approached Rainee. “Ms. Allen, we have a team headed out to Milani’s residence.”

“I want to be there.”

“No doubt, but that would not be prudent. We don’t know how dangerous the situation could be. We will keep you informed.”

“At least tell me, what is the next step?”

“You should know I can’t discuss that.”

“Maybe I watch too many movies, but why not just burst in? They could be inside.”

“If there is the least suspicion that they are there, we will do just that.”

“Agent, I know I sound obvious, but the longer you wait, the greater the chances are you won’t catch them— or the money.”

“Yes. We are aware of that.”

“Fine.”

“Please let us do our job. This type of operation is not new to us. I assure you, we have the best and most experienced agents working on it.”

“Oh, I have no doubt of that.”

Agent Harrington could tell that Rainee was impatient. He cleared his throat and excused himself to get back to work.

Rainee sat down to call Martin and bring him up to date.

He told her how much he loved her and insisted she stay out of the way of Interpol. Yet, Martin knew better of his wife. Nothing was going to get in her way.

With most of the agents out of the room, Rainee left the building. She hailed a taxi and gave the driver Milani’s apartment building address. As she neared, she requested he drive around the corner to drop her off. If Interpol was sitting in a car watching the building, she might be recognized.

She walked toward the building. Fortuitously, a store selling women’s clothing was a few doors down. Rainee went in and bought a new jacket, hat, and sunglasses. Then, put her old jacket into the store’s bag.

Diagonally across from the apartment building was a café. *What a stroke of luck*, thought Rainee. She sat down and ordered a cappuccino. The Interpol unmarked black sedan was positioned directly across from the building. She could see two men smoking cigarettes and talking to each other. Neither of the men were watching the entrance.

Really? Rainee rolled her eyes, losing some confidence in this international agency.

She took out her phone and called the number associated with Milani. It rang for a long time.

Just then, she watched the Interpol car drive away. *Where are they going? Oh well, it's just as well they're leaving.*

She stayed in place and watched the apartment building entrance. Her patience paid off. Suddenly, Esposito himself exited the building carrying a briefcase.

Rainee gasped.

She followed well behind him, comfortable that he would not recognize her even if he looked. He never looked around or behind him. He walked confidently, as if he had no worries at all. They walked for several blocks until he entered Banca d'Italia. She waited across the cobblestoned street in the entranceway of a busy store.

The wait seemed unusually long. Finally, the professor emerged from the bank and walked several more city blocks. Rainee kept pace with him across the road.

She observed as the professor entered Veccia Sparita, a neighborhood restaurant.

Rainee dialed Agent Harrington to let him know that Esposito had gone into a bank. The phone was picked up and she heard a simple, "Pronto."

She told him about what she had witnessed. Agent Harrington, obviously upset, raised his voice and said, "Miss Allen, didn't I tell you not to follow him? It's too dangerous. You could be harmed. I simply will not allow you to do this. You must stop. Now!" She was a bit taken aback by the strength of his command.

"Yes, however, I thought this was valuable information for you to have."

"We already have that information! The transaction was to go to an offshore bank account. The Cayman Islands. We already froze it. Miss Allen, we are working this case. We know how to do our job. Your job is to stay out of the way. Per Favore!"

"Okay," she replied. "But why did your men leave their stakeout position, then? Please tell me that. They missed Esposito by two minutes!"

"We have our reasons. They are our reasons, not yours!" he replied. "Frankly, if you had your eyes off your prey for one second, you would have seen our car at the bank. And keep in mind that we were able to intercept the transaction so quickly.

Now, do I have your word that you will stop following Esposito? I am going to assume that you will do that, so I won't have to bring you in for obstructing our investigation. Hello? Hello?"

Rainee had already hung up and was watching a man approach the entrance of the restaurant. He was alone and, quite suspiciously, looking over his shoulder. He was wearing a Fedora and sunglasses. Her eyes narrowed.

She needed to get closer to see who it was. She crossed the street quickly and approached the entranceway.

Just then, the door was opened by a group of young adults entering the restaurant. They were laughing and loud. She carefully looked through the window and was shocked to see Fabrizio. He and the professor hugged each other, slapped each other on the back, and laughed.

Fabrizio turned around at the sound of the group. He saw a woman in the window and looked directly into Rainee's stare. His eyes widened. He quickly turned and jostled through the newly arriving patrons on his way to the door.

Fabrizio yelled, "Antonio! It is the woman!"

The professor quickly followed his partner out of the restaurant.

Rainee pivoted and started running. She couldn't run fast on the cobblestones, so she hurried to the sidewalk, kicked off her pumps, picked them up, then started running as fast as she could. She was running on a wide, brightly lit avenue. It would be difficult to lose them. She turned a corner to go down a darkened side street.

She ran less than two hundred feet and was tackled from behind. She fought as well as she could, ineffectively trying to use her heels as weapons. She was no match for the detective.

Fabrizio finally pulled a struggling Rainee to her feet.

The professor punched her directly in the face and she dropped. Privately, the professor thought that turnabout was fair play. He grinned.

The two men looked around to make sure they were not seen. There appeared to be no one on the dark street, so they picked up Rainee, one on each side. Her face was bloodied from the strike, but it seemed only to be trickling from her nose. They would carry her like she was very drunk and virtually unconscious.

They started down the side street, singing as if they had also had their share of alcohol. It would be a longer walk to the apartment on the side streets. They had no choice but to walk where there were fewer people.

Fifty-One

Joshua went up to Giulietta's hospital room to say goodbye. He had decided that he would not see her again until the trial.

The police had talked with him about having to return for one. He was unhappy about it, but realized that he would have to, in order to help convict the people who kidnapped him. Except for Giulietta, of course. He would do his best to help her during the proceedings because they had developed a somewhat warm relationship.

He knew he would miss her, but he also felt resentment and distrust, based on the fact that she was part of the plot to steal from his father. He could never forgive her for that.

Though he would not see her for a long while, he made their goodbye seem temporary and casual by lying. He told her he knew she would recover quickly and that he would see her soon. He gently kissed her cheek and left.

After leaving the hospital, he took a taxi to the Verona Porta Nuova Train Station, bought his ticket and boarded the first train to Rome. He had enough money for the train and a couple of taxis, but not much else. He had better find Rainee quickly

The train ride would give him a few hours to think about all that had happened and to figure out a plan to find Rainee. The train left the station on time and Joshua settled back to think. He was deep in sleep within three minutes.

The conductor's loud announcement that the train was arriving in Rome woke him up with a start. He disembarked, walked out of the front of the station and grabbed a taxi to go to Milani's apartment. He was confident that he would find Rainee somewhere near there.

Fifty-Two

Rainee regained consciousness lying on a bed in an empty bedroom. Her head was pounding with pain and she was tied, spread-eagle to the headboard and the footboard. For a couple of confusing moments, she could not recall what happened or why she was in pain. Eventually, she remembered.

She yelled out to Fabrizio, but heard a different voice respond. "Go back to sleep, Sleeping Beauty. It's much quieter when you are sleeping." She knew that voice.

"Professor? Professor Esposito? Is that you?"

No response. Her head was throbbing with pain. "Answer me, please. Is that you?"

A moment later, the door opened, and the professor stood there smiling.

"Thought you could outsmart me, eh? I don't know who the hell you think you are, but you won't be around to see how this thing ends. You have been a thorn in everyone's ass since this started and that has to stop!"

"Professor, please. Let me go. I won't say anything to the police. I don't care about anything else. Joshua is free and unharmed, so you can keep the money and go free."

"Sure. You expect me to believe that? It's already too late, Ms. Allen. You or Joshua will make sure I rot in prison. The boy has known me for over five years. He trusted me. He even liked me, and you know what? I liked him too. I did. His kidnapping was nothing more than a means to an end. I am actually glad that no real harm came to him. I can take some comfort in that while I'm living in luxury. In a place you will never know. No one will."

Rainee winced at the pain. "Professor, do you have any strong analgesics here? Extra-strength aspirin? I am in real pain. My face hurts from the punch. Please, Professor Esposito, please?"

He smiled and closed the door.

"Hello? Professor, can you hear me? Is anybody there?"

Nothing.

She wiggled her wrists, trying to loosen the knots. Her right wrist seemed to have a minor effect on the knot. It relaxed a little, providing some hope, but not enough to allow her to slip out of the rope. At least not yet. Rainee kept working on that one knot. Her wrist contorted in every direction, with little success.

The professor left the apartment, walked down to the first floor, and slid out the back entrance to take side streets and alleys to a small grocerette two blocks away.

He needed to pick up some food and was very careful to avoid being seen by anyone who might be watching the apartment.

Fifty-Three

"Via del Tempio di Diana 65 in Aventino, per favore." Joshua felt nervous. *Will I find Rainee? Is she all right?*

Joshua paid him the €8 plus a tip, got out and then ducked into the same small café Rainee had sat in hours before. He looked at the address across the street where Milani and perhaps the professor were. He ordered a cup of coffee and watched the door of the building.

He was on his third cup of strong Italian coffee when he saw the professor emerge, moving quickly down the street.

Joshua threw some money down onto his table to pay for his coffee and hurriedly moved outside. He walked in the same direction as the professor but stayed over a hundred feet behind him on the other side of the road.

After several blocks, Dr. Esposito entered a small grocerette.

Joshua waited.

Less than ten minutes later, the professor came out carrying two bags. He started back toward the apartment and took his time, strolling, rather than walking with purpose.

Joshua watched him and let him move a full block ahead before he crossed the road and followed him.

Two blocks later, the professor turned left onto a small side street. Joshua saw his chance and picked up speed until he was engaged in a full-on run. It did not take him long to reach his quarry.

He slammed into the professor.

The older man lunged forward and the two bags went flying. The professor skidded face-down on the pavement, deeply abrading his skin in several places. He was conscious but dazed.

"You fucking bastard! You asshole! You set me up? You arranged my kidnapping? You caused all of us so much pain! And you stole from my father! You are one sick fuck! I should kill you!"

The professor stumbled as he tried to stand up. He had little chance of extricating himself from the situation.

"You don't have that killer instinct, Joshua. Now, your mother, Rainee... that's another story. She'd kill me to protect you... without hesitation." Then he mumbled, "Nerve to ask me for aspirin, ha!"

In a rage, Joshua picked up a bottle of wine which had fallen intact. He struck the professor squarely in the temple with a loud and satisfying crack. Esposito hit the pavement with his face a second time and lost consciousness.

Joshua stood there shaking. Had he just killed a man? Would he now be the one that ended up incarcerated? But he had one overriding worry: Rainee. How would he find her?

Professor muttered something about asking him for aspirin. Was he talking about Rainee? Maybe she's in the apartment? But how can I get in? Wait. The professor must have the keys!

A short search produced a small ring of keys in the professor's sweater pocket. Joshua took them, then realized he had to do something with the body. He grabbed the ankles of his former mentor and dragged him into some sparse bushes. That would not hide him for long, but maybe just enough for him to get away.

A quick toss of the scattered groceries and he was on his way.

He reached the apartment building, opened the front door and entered. He found mailboxes in the foyer with one marked *#4 Milani.*

Do I dare enter? What if Milani is in there? But I can't afford to wait anymore, especially if Rainee is in there.

He climbed the stairs and gently knocked on the door. No answer. He knocked a little harder. Nothing. Emboldened, he tried each of the keys until one turned and he felt a click. He turned the doorknob and entered the living room.

He moved quietly across the carpeted room and stepped on a small piece of plastic. It made a click sound and he froze.

"Professor? Professor? Is that you?"

Joshua heard his mother's weak voice and ran into the adjacent bedroom.

"Rainee! Oh my God, Rainee!" yelled Joshua as his gaze fell upon the restraints holding her down. "Shit! I'll get you out of those!"

"The professor left a while ago. Better hurry before he gets back. Oh. Joshua. It's so good to see you!"

"Don't worry about the professor, Rainee. I don't think he'll be bothering us."

Rainee looked at Joshua quizzically.

"I'll tell you later. Let's get you untied and get out of here."

He leaned over her to give her a quick hug, then ran into the small kitchen and rummaged through some drawers until he found a knife. A long moment later, Rainee was free.

She was bloodied and still in pain but felt good to know she would be safe very soon.

Joshua said, "Let's go!"

Rainee reached for her shoes.

He responded, "Hurry. I'll be in the living room to make sure no one comes in."

Too late. The door opened and Fabrizio came in.

"Detective Piscitelli! What are you doing here?"

When she heard Joshua call out Fabrizio's name, Rainee froze.

The detective leapt at Joshua. He easily knocked the knife out of his grip and started swinging.

Rainee frantically scanned the bedroom for some sort of weapon. Anything she could use to overpower Fabrizio.

The room was fairly spartan. Bed, bureau, desk and— *the chair!*

Rainee grabbed the wooden chair, lifted it over her head and carried it into the living room.

Her first sight was Fabrizio's back. He was holding Joshua tightly around the neck.

Joshua was struggling to extricate himself. He took hold of three of the detective's fingers and pulled them back, until Fabrizio had no choice but to let go.

As he did, he shoved Joshua, causing him to tumble backward and fall.

Fabrizio pulled his gun and aimed it at his adversary.

Joshua was wobbling to a standing position.

The door opened and Professor Esposito, blood oozing from his head, staggered into the room.

Fabrizio pivoted suddenly surprised to see him.

Rainee smashed the wooden chair down onto the detective's head. The gun went off.

Fabrizio collapsed, unconscious.

Something slammed into the professor's chest. He fell. His last sight was of Rainee and Joshua embracing.

Joshua took off his belt and knelt over the detective.

At Rainee's urging, the two fled the apartment, only to find an unmarked black sedan stationed on the street. The same agents were inside, smoking unfiltered cigarettes.

Rainee and Joshua started talking at the same time, telling the story.

The officers had Joshua stop so Rainee could tell the story. When they understood, they called it in.

Soon after, Agent Harrington entered the scene to find one bloodied body lying on the living room floor, and one unconscious detective with his hands bound very tightly with a leather belt, the result of Joshua's handiwork.

Fifty-Four

At the station, Rainee and Joshua were asked to give their depositions separately. Both gave the same account of what happened in the apartment. They both swore that Detective Piscitelli entered the apartment, struggled with Joshua and inadvertently shot his own uncle.

The agents drilled down to the most minute details, making sure that their stories coincided. They found it difficult to believe that the well-respected detective would kidnap Rainee and try to kill her and the boy.

Even Agent Harrington met the information with some skepticism. However, he had no choice but to accept the testimony once ballistics returned. The bullet came from Fabrizio's police-issued Beretta service weapon and gunshot residue covered his right hand.

Joshua's fingerprints were not on the gun. The crime scene was just as they claimed.

During that interview Rainee revealed to Harrington the picture she had been carrying: a younger Piscitelli, with a younger Esposito, defiantly holding the flag of the Red Brigade. It took nearly an hour for her to make her statement. By the end, she was tired.

Getting up to finally leave Harrington's office, she asked the detective, "Is there a place I could lie down for a bit? At least, until Joshua has completed his deposition?"

"Oh, certainly, Ms. Allen. Just follow me." He opened the door for her and she stepped into the outer office.

Rainee's jaw dropped open.

Ricky was there in a special reclining wheel chair with two IV poles attached and hoses seemingly going everywhere. He was flanked by a male caregiver and a woman fussing over him.

That must be Deborah.

Ricky had not seen Rainee yet.

She was barely able to speak. Tears welled up in her eyes and spilled down her cheeks.

"Ricky!" she whispered. She cleared her throat and repeated, "Ricky!"

Ricky looked up.

The two stared at each other until Ricky said, "Oh my God, Rainee."

She went to him. She bent down to hug him and they held onto each other tightly. A deluge of tears from both of them mixed together.

"Thank you for saving my boy, Rain. Thank you."

"He's so special, Ricky. He really is." She turned to Deborah. "You must be Deborah. Thank you for raising such a great kid." They hugged.

"Dad! Mom!" Joshua had finished his statement. He ran to his parents, hugging them both. "Boy, am I glad to see you two!"

"Not nearly as glad as we are to see you. Both of you!"

All three of them stood there hugging and crying happy tears.

Deborah held Joshua at arm's length. "Let me look at you. Are you all right? You're face looks pretty banged up!"

"It is, Mom. It hurts just to smile, but I can't help it right now. I am *so* glad to see you both!"

Ricky said, "I just wish I could kiss you somewhere on that face, but I'm afraid of hurting you. Here. Just a small one on the forehead. Is that all right, Josh?"

"Sure, Dad. Please."

They spent the entire day at Interpol talking to agents, filling out forms, and running press gauntlets. Ricky refused to leave his son's side.

Joshua was told he should stay in Rome for at least a week, as there would be more questions and more forms to fill out. He agreed. Besides, he needed a new passport. And more than that, he needed the rest. He looked forward to resuming his life, but he was not ready to go home yet. Arlington seemed like a million miles away.

Rainee was also happy to stay for whatever time the agents thought she should. She missed her daughter and her husband, but here was an opportunity to get to know her son. He was such a mature and smart young man, and he was so very handsome. She beamed with pride.

Joshua had gone through a very harrowing experience that would make its impact known sooner or later. When the initial happiness and relief of surviving ended, there would be emotional fallout. She wanted to be there to help him through it as best she could.

Rainee had left him when he needed her once before. She would not do it again.

Epilogue

The mood was light, yet poignant. Each of the people in the room reflected on the past ten days in their own ways. Different stories. Different experiences. Different emotions. But all shared the overwhelming emotion of happiness to make it through the experience alive and be together with the people they loved.

Ricky provided the hotel suite. It was magnificently furnished like Rainee's Venice hotel. Grand in every detail.

The considerable living room space in the center of the suite featured exquisite textiles with curtains in matching colors. The furniture was spacious and comfortable, elegant and refined. The great table in the center suite presented a large bowl of fruit, a platter of finger foods, several glorious-looking desserts and lots of wine.

It was not long before Rainee, Deborah and even Joshua were feeling the effects of a bottle of red Refosco, an expensive, sought-after wine from the eastern hills of Friuli. Ricky wanted badly to join them, but he was not allowed to mix alcohol with his multitude of pills. He just sat back and reveled in their blissful emotional release.

Joshua could not stop talking about his captivity and some of the horrifying experiences he had. Things he had witnessed and things he had heard. He explained about Giulietta, adding that he sincerely hoped she would heal quickly. He was telling his stories so breathlessly, it was as if he had a time limit to get out all the details.

At one point, Ricky said, "Josh, come up for air! You should eat a little something. I can see that you've lost a bunch of weight. We've got to get some meat on those bones."

They all went to the table and partook of the delicacies. They were famished. Everything was delicious. Ricky had done well when he arranged ahead to order all the food and drink. He could not do enough to ensure their comfort and happiness.

Rainee asked Joshua, "What happened to your friend, Zack? How come he's not here for the festivities?"

"Agent Harrington told me Zack got a call from a hospital in the States saying his grandmother, who had been really ill, had a major stroke and it didn't look good. His parents were camping somewhere and unreachable."

A concerned Rainee said, "Oh my, that's awful."

Joshua started laughing. "Yeah, well, what's really awful was that it was a ruse. Apparently, Zack was so upset that I was missing, he was trying to arrange his flights so he could stay and help search for me.

But the professor wanted him out of the way and not complicating the situation, so he arranged the call. See? I was right after all. I always knew the professor liked Zack more than me."

Everyone laughed.

"Wait, there's more. In an earlier conversation with the professor, Zack had mentioned his concern for his grandmother. He also told us that his parents were away and unreachable. The professor must have been listening well. Zack fell for it and took the earliest flight out of Rome." He added, "Can you imagine his face when he showed up at her supposed death bed? I would love to have been there." Joshua chuckled. "His grandmother must have been even more surprised."

"So, he's okay?" Deborah asked.

"Yeah, I spoke with him from the police station. He was really relieved to hear my voice."

The discussion also touched upon Fabrizio and the professor. Everyone wondered what would become of the likeable detective, who seemed so helpful and genuine until he kidnapped Rainee and tried to kill Joshua at the apartment.

Rainee said that she badly wanted to hear that he was sentenced to a long prison term. She would feel safer that way. She added, "Agent Harrington informed me that after Piscitelli was arrested, a one-way airplane ticket to Bali was found in one of his pockets. That really sealed his fate. They didn't need much more to prove his involvement with the money."

It turned out the apartment registered under the fictitious name of Paolo Milani was just another safe house for the Red Brigade. Rainee laughed. "Another reason it didn't have a cozy, comfy feel."

There was a knock on the door. Joshua jumped up from the sofa and went to get it. He said with a smile, "More food, I bet."

It was Martin and little Jana.

Jana peeked in the door and screamed, "Mummy!" then dropped out of Martin's arms. She ran to a surprised Rainee, wrapped her arms around her neck and gave her a giant hug, accompanied by lots of kisses.

Rainee flew into Martin's arms. Tears that had been withheld all day erupted as Martin's arms enveloped his wife. They held each other tightly.

He lifted her chin and looked into her eyes. "You are an amazing woman, Rainee.

She smiled. "Funny, Fabrizio said that to me. Seems like such a long time ago."

"I'm so proud of you. But don't you ever do this again. I— *we* love you too much to come that close to losing you."

All Rainee could do was nod and snuggle her head into Martin's neck.

Joshua walked over.

Rainee straightened and gestured. "Martin, meet my son Joshua. Joshua, Martin."

Martin looked into his eyes and saw Rainee. It was almost uncanny how much he looked like her.

Joshua held out his hand.

Martin pulled him into a hug. "Joshua, I am so very happy to finally meet you," he said. "You gave us quite a scare. We're all grateful that you are all right."

"Yes, sir. Thank you very much."

Martin smiled at Joshua's polite manner, then turned and walked to Ricky. "I'm also pleased to make your acquaintance, Ricky. You have raised a remarkable son."

The two men hugged. "It's great to meet you, Martin."

Martin turned toward Deborah and said, "Deborah, I presume? Maybe I should have directed that compliment to you."

Deborah smiled. "Nowadays, it takes a village." They all laughed and nodded.

There was a tug on Rainee's slacks. Jana said, "Mummy, who are these people?"

Rainee picked up her little girl and walked over to Joshua. "Sweetheart, I want to introduce you to your brother. This is Joshua."

"Hi!" Her pipsqueak voice made Joshua smile.

He asked, "Can I get a hug?" With a smile that stretched from ear to ear, Jana nodded.

He picked her up in his arms and squeezed her tightly. "I've always wanted a little sister. May I show you around this place?"

With a wide grin, she nodded and off they went to explore the enormous suite.

Martin fell comfortably into the conversation and atmosphere. Mostly, he kept his eyes on his wife, grateful she had survived.

Rainee explained to Martin how she had emerged from the interrogation room and, to her astonishment, saw Ricky, who was flanked by his wife and his attendant.

Ricky chuckled. "When I found out Josh was okay, all I wanted to do was to dance... and dammit, they wouldn't let me!"

Everyone laughed.

Rainee said, "Didn't Mark Twain say something like, 'Humor is tragedy plus time'? It's amazing we can all sit around here and laugh."

Ricky said, “Perhaps it’s just a bit like mass comedic hysteria. But boy, has it helped ease the tension.”

Throughout the afternoon and evening, Deborah stayed by her husband’s side, sharing duties with the private duty nurse and tending to his every physical need, of which there were many. He was filled with relief and gratitude that he had his son back. Ricky was not even aware of his own pain and discomfort. He just felt incredibly content.

Every so often, Joshua would walk over to Deborah and give her a peck on the cheek and a hug. Then he’d say, “I love, you, Mom.” Each time he did though, he felt a little uneasy doing it in front of the woman that gave birth to him. He knew Rainee understood, but still, it probably made her a little uncomfortable. He was thankful for all she had done for him. He did not want to upset her in any way.

Joshua absentmindedly put his hand into his pocket, felt something and pulled out the Italian horn given to him by Professor Esposito for good luck.

His quiet chuckle turned into a loud laugh. When everyone turned to him, he related the story of the gift, then added, “Turns out I had good luck with me the whole time. But I don’t think the professor did.”

Throughout the hours, there was laughter and tears and many more stories. But mostly, there was gratitude.

Rainee felt profound love in the air. She looked around the room and smiled, reflecting on these people and the events that led up to this moment. This was a group of people who would not lose touch ever again.

-END-

Acknowledgements

We wish to thank our spouses, Michael Grossman and Janet Jaroslow, without whose patience, support, love, and belief in our dream, would have made this an impossible venture.

Our respective children; Rachel and Zachary (Lauren), and Jenna and Evan (Bernard), whose love fills us both with pride and joy.

Our editor and teacher, Harvey Stanbrough, for helping us to perfect and tighten the story.

Joyce Keating, literary agent, whose patience, diligence, and loyalty has been so appreciated.

Shera Cohen, who provided an incredible experience in accruing background research on a memorable trip to Italy for me (Lauren) and also knowing the right questions for the interview in the back of this book.

Grazie to Antonio Giannone for making sure our Italian verbiage was, in fact, correct.

Thanks again to Evan Jaroslow for creating the cover art. Your musical and artistic abilities always astonish us.

We are indebted to our Beta readers: Hana Axmannová, Zachary Grossman, Sondra Shapiro, Shera Cohen and Mary Ann Cunningham. Your input was invaluable and we will be forever grateful.

And lastly, a big thanks to Jonathan and his staff at the Coffee Exchange, for letting me (Lauren) sit for hours with just one cup of coffee.

Interview with the Authors

Questions by Shera Cohen, In the Spotlight, Inc.

SC: Why did you decide to write the book? To write it together?

LBG: *There was a tremendous response to "The Golden Peacock" - the first Rainee Allen mystery. It just seemed a natural progression to continue with a protagonist who people liked.*

As far as writing it with Bernie— he had been a big contributor to the first book. I would write several chapters, then send it to him. He made some great edits and suggestions, which helped steer the course of my novel. Besides, I kinda like my big brother.

BJ: *Me too, Laur. Writing a novel with another person is both easier and more difficult than writing alone. It is easier because you can share ideas and help each other keep the story on track. It is more difficult because the story changes and evolves while in each author's hands.*

SC: How do two people write a novel together? Does that fact that you are siblings, coming from the essentially same background, add or subtract to the writing experience?

LBG: *It was certainly a new experience for me. I was so used to writing alone. This time I wrote only from Rainee's point-of-view (POV), and Bernie wrote from Joshua's POV. Since my background is theatre, I write a lot of dialogue. Bernie's background is business writing and he writes a lot of narrative. So, each time we swapped chapters, I would add dialogue to his writings, and he would add narrative to mine. I hope this created a seamless delivery to the readers.*

I do believe that since we are siblings, it added to the experience. We laugh a lot when we're together and we laugh a lot when we are separated by 1,500 miles.

BJ: *Having both male and female perspectives is advantageous as each author writes from their personal perception to help make each character more believable and more real. As Lauren said, we actually split the writing up by each writing the characters from their perspective gender.*

I, too, believe being siblings worked well for us both. We are very similar in the way we write and in the way we approach storytelling. I couldn't imagine writing with anyone else.

SC: Did you decide the ending before you started and then work toward it?

LBG: *Personally, I have never worked that way. I just start typing and, like a puzzle, the pieces just come together. I hope, in a good way.*

Currently, I am renovating a room in my house. When I began, I had no idea what I wanted to do with it. But once I found the right pillow, I could envision the rest of the room around it. For me, writing is like that. Piece by piece, coming together.

BJ: *We knew there would be a kidnapping of Rainee's son, and she would become embroiled in his rescue. It was interesting to see how the details unfolded as we worked it out.*

S.C. Which came first, the characters or the story? Or simultaneously?

LBG: *In "The Golden Peacock," Rainee mentioned to her best friend Shelley about her greatest fear; meeting the child she gave up when she was twenty-one. It was two paragraphs in the entire novel, and never mentioned again. I wanted Rainee Allen to meet her biological son. And, of course, we had to build a mystery around it.*

BJ: Since it's a Rainee Allen mystery, it was always going to have Rainee as the protagonist. Introducing her son as one of the main characters was an early thought, so I would say the characters *and* the story were developed almost simultaneously.

SC: Are your characters based on real people who either of you know?

LBG: *There tends to be a lot of me in Rainee. Cannot seem to help myself. I ask myself how I would react in this situation. I am a mother and would become a lioness to protect my cubs. Bernie and I liked using names of people we know in this novel, but I don't believe their characterizations are the same. Bernie can speak to his writing of the character Joshua.*

BJ: Rainee Allen is loosely based on Lauren— or at least the woman Lauren dreamed about being (and was, to some degree). Frankly, I suppose there's a little of me in Joshua. But no other characters are based on people we know.

SC: How much research was done on the Brigade?

BJ: *Quite a bit. I was in Italy in the 1980's, during the time that the American General Dozier was in captivity. I was even there (across the street) when he was rescued. I read a lot about the group and their tactics and wanted to bring them into this story.*

LBG: *Bernie did most of the research about them. The Red Brigade existed from 1970-1988. Sadly, with the isolationist ideology that many countries have adapted throughout the world, they are back on the rise again.*

SC: Do you critique each other? Do you edit each other about: particular wording, pace, how to balance narrative with dialog?

LBG: *Yes!*

BJ: *We really spent countless hours on Facetime going over every line— every word. One would write a chapter, then we would go over every detail together. Each of us usually acquiesced when the other felt that there was a better way to write or describe something. That may be the result of being close siblings, but I would say that the writing and edit processes went pretty smoothly.*

SC: How did you decide when and where to place the story?

BJ: *Since we knew that Rainee's son would be one of the main characters, the "when" was a given. The "where" had to be worked out. The timing of the resurgence of the Red Brigade activity helped with both of those considerations.*

LBG: *My research for "The Golden Peacock" began in London. After visiting Italy, it seemed logical to make this setting there. Stay tuned for the next Rainee Allen mystery, which is set in Prague, Czech Republic. It was a great visit!*

SC: How did you know when the story/the plot was done?

BJ: In this story, the resolution of the plot represented a natural and satisfying end of story.

LBG: *My feeling has always been that once you have reached the climatic arc, the denouement follows, and then you can tie it all together with an epilogue. I don't believe the readers want to be belabored by reading past that point. The end is the end!*

About the Authors

Award-winning author Lauren B. Grossman found global success with her debut novel *Once in Every Generation*. Her first Rainee Allen mystery, *The Golden Peacock*, was so well received, that creating a series seemed like a natural progression. First set in London, now Italy, look for the next one to be set in Prague. That Rainee sure gets around.

Ms. Grossman earned her degree in theatre and has performed in, designed sets, directed and produced numerous productions.

Ms. Grossman co-founded, co-published, and co-edited a performing arts newspaper. Because of the success of that newspaper, she and her co-publisher created a weekly radio talk show. She has had articles published and has earned awards for her short stories.

Ms. Grossman resides in Southern Arizona with her husband, two children, a dog and desert tortoise.

This is Bernie Jaroslow's first novel as a co-author. He became a technical writer in the dental industry due to his love of reading and writing short stories. He has authored books on dental technology and many technical articles and is presently employed by a dental product manufacturer where he provides much of the written content for the company's marketing efforts, including eBooks, white papers, weekly blogs, and brochures.

Bernie lives with his wife, Janet, in Louisville, KY and has two grown children, Jenna and Evan. His son, Evan, created the cover art for this book and for the previous Rainee Allen mystery, *The Golden Peacock*.